The Neorealist in Winter

Stories

The Neo

Salvatore Pane

Winner of the Autumn House Fiction Prize

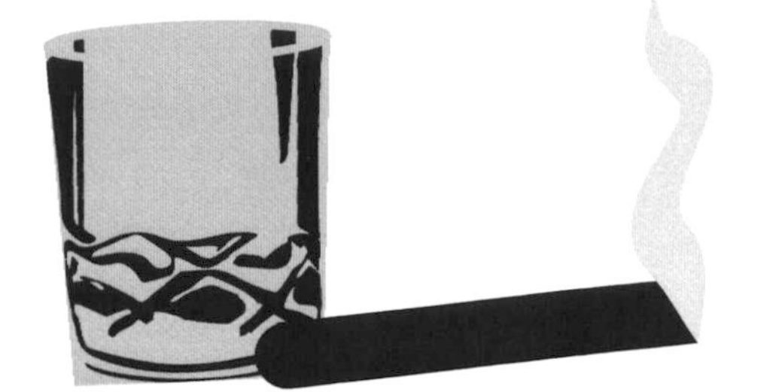

stories

realist in Winter

AUTUMN HOUSE PRESS
PITTSBURGH, PA

The Neorealist in Winter: Stories

Published by Autumn House Press
ISBN: 978-1-637680-78-0

Cover and Design by Joel W. Coggins

Library of Congress Cataloging-in-Publication Data

Names: Pane, Salvatore, author.
Title: The neorealist in winter : stories / Salvatore Pane.
Description: Pittsburgh : Autumn House Press, 2023.
Identifiers: LCCN 2023023118 | ISBN 9781637680780 (paperback) | ISBN 9781637680797 (epub)
Subjects: LCGFT: Short stories.
Classification: LCC PS3616.A3684 N46 2023 | DDC 813/.6--dc23/eng/20230515
LC record available at https://lccn.loc.gov/2023023118

Printed in the United States on acid-free paper that meets the international standards of permanent books intended for purchase by libraries.

Autumn House Press is a nonprofit corporation whose mission is the publication and promotion of poetry and other fine literature. The press gratefully acknowledges support from individual donors, public and private foundations, and government agencies. This book was supported, in part, by the Greater Pittsburgh Arts Council through its Allegheny Arts Revival Grant and the Pennsylvania Council on the Arts, a state agency funded by the Commonwealth of Pennsylvania, and the National Endowment for the Arts. To find out more about how National Endowment for the Arts grants impact individuals and communities, visit www.arts.gov.

For Theresa

Contents

"It was a village that knew nothing beyond its own misery . . . "

—Natalia Ginzburg, *All Our Yesterdays*

"You speak of the old world. This is another world."

—Pietro di Donato, *Christ in Concrete*

The Neorealist in Winter

Stories

The Neorealist in Winter

Jackie knew from Strickland's smile that something had gone wrong. Strickland was optimistic to a fault, always grinning, would happily wave as prison guards strapped him into the electric chair. Whenever things turned bad—like after Phoebe King's review in *The New Yorker* or when Cassavetes forgot to read Jackie's new script—Strickland turned exponentially enthusiastic, the Joker by way of a Ken doll. And that's exactly how he appeared bounding up to Jackie at a table outside Canova, the Piazza del Popolo framed behind him, its obelisk pointed at the gathering clouds.

"Ciao, pal!" Strickland shouted, kissing Jackie on both cheeks even though Strickland was a WASP from Vermont. Jackie forced a smile and stared at his negroni and complimentary snacks. He'd never been to Italy during winter and had expected the snow-kissed avenues of his youth. Instead, December in Rome felt like a New York autumn, and he'd abandoned his heavy down coat at the Hotel de Russie. For Canova, he'd course corrected too far by wearing a lightweight sport coat, and the breeze left him chilled and exposed. It was 1973, and he still didn't know how to dress.

Strickland undid his trench coat and set it over his chair. "I did some digging on Marciano."

Jackie ate a greasy chip. It was after four, almost *aperitivo*, and Canova was already filled with the buzzing denizens of Rome's artiste elite, men and women shouting at each other in a language Jackie Donato still recognized, the muted echo of his Sicilian mother in all those wrung out images—the black house dress, hunched over the stove, on her knees at the Church of the Most Precious Blood—or his father returning home from the Garment District, how he'd gather the men from their building each Saturday for *briscola*.

"He's willing to meet with you," Strickland said. "Marciano. He saw *Are You There, Cugino?* and was blown away."

That, Jackie knew, meant he'd liked it just fine. "Did you set up a meeting with his agent?"

Strickland moved a *tarallo* to his napkin. "Well, it turns out Commendatore Marciano is throwing a party tonight."

"Don't use that word. Nobody uses that word," Jackie told him. "What kind of party?"

Strickland gestured with his hand like an Italian. Strickland was like risotto, Jackie thought, absorbing the flavor of anything nearby. "It's one of these big Roman parties. We've survived this kind of baby kissing a hundred times. It'll be fine."

"So we meet Marciano at his party and book a red-eye home, right?"

"It's not exactly that simple." Strickland judiciously chose an olive and set it next to his *tarallo*. "According to his agent, Marciano's a bit . . . eccentric."

Jackie took a long sip from his negroni.

"He apparently will only engage with a director he doesn't know if he makes it through the entirety of one of his parties."

"You're kidding. And how late do these events go?"

"Depends."

That meant sunup.

"And," Strickland continued, "he only takes a liking to these young directors if he sees them drinking all night."

Jackie rubbed his forehead. "What are you saying?"

"You basically always need to be seen with a drink in your hand. Marciano's an old lion. Hates blow and weed, but thinks it's important to reach the right state of consciousness before having a conversation about art."

"You're telling me I have to drink until sunup?"

"Exactly." Strickland swiped Jackie's negroni and finished it. "So cut it out with these, and let's order some food. We need to establish a base." He snapped his fingers at the waiter.

"Strick, it's three days till Christmas. You know I'm trying to get home, right?"

The sun peeked out from the overcast sky and cast a sliver of pale light across the piazza. Three kids in beanies jumped in and out of the light as Strickland reached across the table and patted Jackie's hand. He still wasn't used to this—how easily men from the world outside the neighborhood demonstrated kindness. "I'm trying, Jackie. I'm really trying."

• • •

At ten, Strickland settled the check and flagged down a cabbie, relaying the address of Pietro Marciano a half-hour away. The cabbie grunted, but soon they were speeding away from the cobblestone of Piazza del Popolo toward the paved roads of the dingy suburbs—built by Mussolini and the fascists, Strickland whispered—and then out of the city altogether, emerging in an affluent neighborhood flush with villas and swaying palm trees that reminded Jackie of Malibu. The cabbie rolled to a stop in front of a stone wall concealing a handful of lit-up villas—vaulted ceilings, high windows, at least three terraces. Live music spilled out, and bodies gathered on the manicured grass, the many balconies, by the pool. Jackie stood on the pavement, hands on hips, staring at the property. He had no idea how he'd get back to his hotel room, let alone New York.

Five years had passed since Jackie finished film school and traded the canyons of Manhattan for the sprawl of LA. And during that time Strickland—the wunderkind producer he met through John Cassavetes who selected one of Jackie's student films for a prestigious award—had convinced him to appear at dozens of Hollywood parties to glad hand and fundraise. Jackie always drank, smoked, and/or snorted too much on these occasions, wondering what his parents or brother would make of these spectacles—of elderly producers publicly performing oral sex on would-be starlets, of food bills eclipsing five figures, the mother Jackie witnessed teaching her daughter how to shoot up. The collision of these two worlds—his childhood on Worth Street fighting over the last of the polenta and the absurd wealth and privilege of the Hollywood set—turned him uneasy and taciturn, longing for the comforts of hanging around Perino's with his other pals from New York who'd made the pilgrimage to LA, how they'd sit around for hours rehashing John Ford and Hitchcock. Jackie didn't know in 1973 how quickly life could change, that in a decade's time after rattling off two masterpieces back-to-back—1976's *A Cabbie's Dilemma* and 1980's *The Last Contender*—he'd purchase a villa exactly like this one in Bel Air, that he'd host similar parties and marry Liza Minnelli, casting her in his ill-fated attempt at a screwball revival, fooling around between takes, snorting coke off her back, how he'd end up in rehab and forgo drugs for the rest of his life. But in Pietro Marciano's villa, Jackie made a beeline for the bar—he would've done so even if he hadn't promised to drink all night—and ordered a negroni, feeling calm only when the cold glass was in his hands, moisture wetting his fingers.

The outdoor bar overlooked the evening's entertainment, a small stage where an Italian band played music evoking early Beatles or Stones. The bartender could've explained they were called I Camaleonti, mildly famous in Europe for a few songs played non-diegetically during Pietro Marciano's films. But Jackie didn't ask and instead watched the Italians dancing by the stage, pumping their arms with abandon. And it was this moment when everything changed, when Jackie glanced up at the villa on the other side of the stage and through an open window locked eyes with Pietro Marciano descending the stairs. Dressed more like Castro than a titan of Italian cinema, Pietro Marciano emerged on the opposite landing in olive fatigues and tan slacks. He was still muscular and cut a dashing figure with his white beard and lit cigar, tumbler of brown liquor in hand.

"What do you think?" Strickland asked.

Jackie wanted to say what was expected of him—Marciano looked the part of a charismatic old lion. But there was something gnawing at him, some inner voice Jackie had failed again and again to silence. The perennially frightened voice of his mother, how she would whisper, "Beware that man. He's the devil." Jackie couldn't explain why in that moment he felt his mother calling out to him, but he couldn't deny it. He despised the Catholic superstitions of the old neighborhood yet couldn't carve himself free from his past. The devil. It was so stupid his face flooded with shame.

The moment ended, and Pietro Marciano disappeared in the crowd, the half-moon suspended above like a blade.

• • •

During an interview after the 1969 premiere of *Are You There, Cugino?* at the Chicago International Film Festival, Roger Ebert stood up in the audience and asked Jackie Donato to name his influences. It was a flat question, the kind Ebert would derisively term a "Big Mac" later, empty calories lacking nourishment. But Jackie stiffened behind the table beneath the shrouded movie screen, Strickland on his left. He took Ebert's question seriously, wanting to pay homage to the many voices that cracked open the door for him. "Welles was the big bang for a lot of us," he said into the microphone. "And John Cassavetes too. He's basically been my mentor since grad school. Then there's John Ford. Mizoguchi. Oh, and when I was a kid, Channel 4 ran these terrific subtitled Italian movies. *Bicycle Thieves. Paisan. La Strada.*" He trailed off, aware he was omitting a particularly formative film, and hoped the crowd hadn't caught the break in his voice, that Ebert was satisfied and would let the question drop.

Jackie had first seen the omitted *La Penitenza* in 1954, sprawled on the floor next to his older brother Joey who had commandeered the TV. It was his brother who trained him to love movies and introduced Jackie to the shining amphitheater of Loew's Canal and larger-than-life figures like Brando, Gary Cooper, Liz Taylor. A very different film from those pictures, *La Penitenza* was firmly entrenched in the Italian neorealist tradition established after World War II, when Italy's greatest directors traded the discarded husks of Cinecittà's backlot studios—founded by Mussolini and the fascists years prior—for the bombed-out streets of Rome. Gone were the glitz and glamour of Mussolini's propaganda films, replaced by real people in real streets following gritty scripts that closely aligned with their own lives. *La Penitenza* was Marciano's breakthrough on the international stage, and it followed Marcello, a fascist municipality officer, navigating the poverty of post-War Rome. The newly unemployed protagonist hunts each of Rome's day labor sites for work, but someone always recognizes him from his fascist days and casts him out, often violently. After his wife and son abscond north with a Milanese industrialist, the defeated Marcello seeks out a priest at the Basilica di Santa Maria. Marcello explains that he only joined the fascists because he had to, that he needed to feed his family, that he couldn't join the resistance because he couldn't risk leaving them without a breadwinner. In an unexpected twist that shocked young Jackie and his preteen brother, the priest refuses to forgive him and spits on his shoes. Tears ran down his older brother's cheeks as Marcello climbed the bell tower and hurled himself to the pavement below.

Before Marcello's death, Jackie thought movies existed to pass the time. *La Penitenza* taught him that films could also hurt you. It taught Jackie Donato to look beyond what was merely onscreen. What kind of man dreamed up *La Penitenza*? And who pointed the camera and shouted action with intent to hurt, not to heal?

That man was Pietro Marciano, and the respected minds of *Cahiers du Cinéma*—including both André Bazin and Truffaut—wrote that he was as talented as his neorealist peers, as De Sica and Rossellini and Visconti, names that would guide European cinema for decades to come. And yet, the fifties were not kind to Pietro Marciano, and not one of his films—not *Il Mare non Bagna Napoli* which took an Anna Maria Ortese story for its inspiration, nor *Poveri e Coraggioso* and its depiction of labor strikes starring the miscast Leopoldo Trieste, and not even *Milano Centrale* with Eva Marie Saint and Rod Steiger on loan from Columbia—proved a financial or critical hit. By the sixties, Marciano was labeled a one-hit wonder, juiced in his youth by the energy that flowed freely through Italy after the War. And so, Marciano had no choice but to accept a shoestring budget in 1967 and fly coach to the Tabernas Desert to film the spaghetti western *They'll Run Out of Coffins When Chico Comes to Town* starring Maurizio Merli. *Chico* was envisioned by its financiers—plastic magnates from the north—as a rote cash-in on Sergio Leone's Eastwood westerns, intended for the second-run theatres littered across rural Italy. Yet somehow, Pietro Marciano produced the rare western that hit not only with audiences but with critics too. Unlike most westerns, Marciano drenched *Chico* in contemporary Italian pop, piping in I Camaleonti's surfer ballad "Unchain My Heart" as Chico first entered the Rusty Nail Saloon and pumped lead into sixteen mustachioed land pirates. Neon-coated and overstuffed with blood, rape, and gore, Marciano was celebrated as the reborn auteur of the pop-art cowboy, and he capitalized on his rekindled success by releasing three more westerns in the next thirty months—*Chico Shoots the Living and Buries the Dead, Dig Your Grave or Don't; Either Way You Die*, and *Chico's Back and So Is His Shotgun*.

Jackie ran out on opening night for each of these films, and each time he left the theatre disappointed and angry. He didn't see the "French New Wave angst" that *Cahiers du Cinéma* insisted upon, nor was he impressed by the juxtaposition of Wild West violence with the melodies of Italian rock. Jackie sat stupefied through each of these films, blinking at other viewers hooting and hollering as Chico let loose with a Gatling gun on a Tijuana whorehouse. What happened to the Pietro Marciano of old, he wondered, the man who made *La Penitenza* and cracked open his brother's heart?

Even though it was a crucial omission, Jackie would never admit to Roger Ebert and the crowd gathered at the 1969 Chicago International Film Festival that he'd been influenced by Pietro Marciano. And for hours after the panel—even on the flight back to LA, drinking celebratory martinis with Strickland—Jackie couldn't shake the feeling that he'd betrayed his artistic sensibilities in some fundamental way. Who could say if he would have enrolled in film school if he hadn't seen *La Penitenza*? And where would he be then?

When they landed in LA after the premiere, Strickland insisted on a victory dinner at Dominick's, the first sign that bad news lurked on the horizon. Strick scooped the marrow from his bone with a tiny spoon, grinning all the while. "I want you to know, Jackie, that what I'm about to say isn't coming from me. I have nothing but affection for your brother. He's a lovable scamp, and he's carved out a place in my heart."

Jackie set down his spoon and picked up his bourbon.

"But you have to send him back to New York."

Dominick's was packed that night, with men in suits and hippie cast-offs, women in mod-dresses charming producers. What mystified Jackie—and would continue to confound him for his entire life—was how suddenly the tenement on Worth Street could summon him home, if not in body, then in mind and spirit. His childhood didn't care that he was consuming bone marrow surrounded by actors. His childhood didn't care if *Are You There, Cugino?* had successfully premiered in Chicago. His childhood would always come for him. And it would savor its pound of flesh.

"What did Joey do this time?" Jackie asked.

"Well . . ." Strickland flashed his straight teeth. "He talked Cassavetes into bringing him to a party at Jeannie Berlin's."

"And?"

Strickland finished his bone marrow. "He got into a fistfight with Peter Falk and put him in the hospital."

Jackie immediately knew this was true and that Falk was the wronged party. His older brother had been nothing but a burden since arriving in LA a year earlier. Jackie paid for Joey's way out west—had even covered his bail for a gambling charge back East and agreed to host him until he got settled. Since then, he borrowed $10,000 from Jackie, sold Don Sutherland a bad batch of cocaine laced with thallium sulfate, and was banned for life from Perino's, La Paloma, and Musso and Frank's. Jackie had tried reigniting his older brother's love of film and had even taken him as his plus one to the Hollywood premiere of *The Battle of Algiers*, but Joey fell asleep midway through and mumbled, "It was kids' stuff," when pressed on the drive home.

"What happened?" Jackie asked Strickland.

"Cassavetes says they were fighting over a girl. Next thing he knew, your brother tossed Falk through a glass table and lacerated his face. They had to halt production on *Castle Keep*, the new Lancaster movie with Falk. So now Columbia's involved, and they want your brother's head on a spike. They could blackball you for all we know." Strickland smiled. "Look, everyone in town loves you. *Are You There, Cugino?* is going to be a critical hit, and you're the next big thing. But you have to ship your brother back home. He's going to kill your career before it even gets started. Every person out here who didn't come from money has to scale back contact with their family. It's the business, Jackie. I haven't seen my mother in three years. I share this as an achievement."

The problem Jackie would never untangle was how the same blood and environment could produce such different results. His older brother adored films growing up, had screamed as John Wayne chased villains across the plains. And yet, he grew out of it by high school and traded afternoons at the movies with Jackie for a bad crowd who drank at the Mulberry Street Bar every night. He'd never held a job for more than three weeks and was destined, according to their mother, "for an early grave or prison." How was this possible when Jackie won a scholarship to NYU where he was hand-chosen by John Cassavetes himself? Jackie sensed that Strickland was right, that Joey would drag him back into the gutter if he weren't careful. So, when he returned that night to his rental nestled toward the bottom of the Hollywood Hills, Jackie didn't protest when Strickland called a repair man to change the locks. Together, they wrote an amicable but stern letter explaining the situation, that Joey had to return home, if not for his sake then at least for Jackie's. They left it in the mailbox along with a sizable check. Then they hid for three nights in Ben Gazzara's Malibu beach pad. When they returned, the letter was gone but not the check. Four years had passed, and still the brothers had not spoken. A blessing, Strickland told him. An honest-to-goodness blessing.

• • •

Two negronis. Four negronis. Five negronis. Six. It was three a.m., and I Camaleonti had returned for their second set, a hundred Italians gathered around the stage. Strickland urged Jackie to slow down, but he couldn't help himself and took a sip whenever he felt uncomfortable. He felt like an outsider everywhere, too much of a working-class wop for Hollywood, too pretentious and learned for the old neighborhood, and too much of an ugly American for Rome. This last revelation hit him hardest. Wasn't this the homeland? And if he didn't feel at home here, would he ever feel comfortable anywhere other than behind the lens of a camera? His mother had begged him to return for Christmas, her beloved son who she had not seen in a year (!), her beloved son who had not seen his own brother in four. She'd promised to reunite her two precious bambini and had talked Joey into returning from Teaneck for the feast of the seven fishes to finally make peace with his younger brother. Wasn't that wonderful, his mother pleaded into the phone. Wasn't that grand?

Jackie ordered his seventh negroni and wondered if any of it even mattered. He could mend fences with his brother, but then it would only be a matter of time until Joey asked him for another "loan," before he popped up uninvited in LA, before he knocked up a hooker or helped a TV cowboy overdose. Why bother?

Strickland slapped Jackie on the back, turning him ever so slightly toward Pietro Marciano, sitting on the other side of the stage by a group of young hangers-on, torches spitting fire into the night sky. Each member of Marciano's crew held a glass of anisette, and they went around in a circle toasting the man *Cahiers du Cinéma* deemed the savior of the western. "He's insatiable," Strickland said. "You've matched him drink for drink, and you can barely stand, and he looks like he's barely started."

"Fucking wop," Jackie muttered.

"Jesus Christ." Strickland glanced around. "Let's find you an espresso."

Jackie followed the vibrating outline of Strickland inside. They wouldn't have even needed Pietro Marciano if it weren't for Phoebe King's negative review in *The New Yorker*. She'd loved *Are You There, Cugino?* and had written about it in glowing terms. But the financers of Jackie's second feature,

Spiritual Pain, insisted on previewing a rough cut to critics in SoHo months before it was ready. His second film was a meditation on adolescence in the mean streets of Manhattan's lower east side starring Gian Maria Volonté in a role modeled after his older brother. *Spiritual Pain* was violent and gritty, purged of the tricolor sheen Jackie cast over Italian America in *Are You There, Cugino?* King despised it—"a self-indulgent mess following unlikable characters pursuing dirty deeds done dirt cheap"—and now the studio had developed a case of cold feet. They hated the ending that killed off Gian Maria Volonté in a meaningless back-alley scuffle while his younger brother—played as a sniveling doofus by John Cazale—escaped Manhattan once and for all. There was even talk about shelving the film altogether.

It was at this critical moment when Strickland first evoked the name of Pietro Marciano, explaining that the neorealist turned western savant had transformed himself into a kingmaker abroad who could easily land *Spiritual Pain* on any number of prestigious European festival circuits and had already performed this favor for any number of notable names— Bogdanovich, De Palma, Bob Rafelson, even John Cassavetes himself. "Cassavetes?" Jackie asked while smoking hash in Jim Brown's mansion. "Call and ask about it," Strick said. A few years earlier, they could have gone directly to Cassavetes for help. But ever since the disastrous release of his film *Husbands*, Cassavetes had more than enough money problems of his own. That's how quickly everything could change in Hollywood, Jackie knew. One minute, you're on top of the world, starring in *Rosemary's Baby*. The next, you're a leper.

"Jackie baby, how you doing?" Cassavetes said after Jackie finally got through to him by phone. "When are you going to visit our beach house in Athens? Gena misses you, kid. We've got a bottle of ouzo with your greasy wop name on it."

"John." Even then, a few days before his trip to Rome, it took all of Jackie's restraint not to say *Mr. Cassavetes*. Instead, he thanked *John* profusely for the invitation and gently steered him to business. "Did Strickland tell you about our studio problem?"

"Sure, kid. Don't let the suits intimidate you. They always trot out the same fucking song and dance."

"Well, Strickland got us a meeting with Pietro Marciano about landing our picture on the European festival circuit. I need to know. Is this bullshit? Did you really go to Marciano for help?"

For the briefest of intervals Cassavetes was silent, and this confirmed everything Jackie Donato needed to know. "Sure, Jackie boy," he said, voice slower. "I flew to Rome to ask your countryman for help. Marciano's connected. He put up some funding for *Faces* and steered it to Venice."

Steered it to Venice, Jackie knew, meant the Venice Film Festival where John Cassavetes's *Faces* was nominated for a Golden Lion and resurrected his career. "But what did you have to do for him?"

"I didn't have to blow him or anything. For fuck's sakes, Jackie. The imagination on this kid!" He coughed into the receiver. "I talked up one of the Chico sequels in *Variety*, helped convince United Artists to release it wide in the States." Another pause. "Maybe I was responsible for talking Farley Granger into playing the heavy. Old guys give us money; we give old guys cred."

What bothered Jackie most about international phone calls—even more than the cost—was the static. It didn't sound right and was somehow both tinnier and thicker, like Jackie was actually calling from the moon. "But you didn't actually like those Chico pictures, right?" he asked.

"Oh," Cassavetes laughed, "of course not. Nobody fucking likes 'em. But we all gotta kiss the ring occasionally. That's what this whole house of cards is built on, pal."

Drunk off negronis, Jackie could barely reconcile that conversation with the reality of standing inside Marciano's home, staring at a fresco on the ceiling next to Strickland. The sun had risen and most of the revelers had finally left. Jackie didn't know much about frescoes, and neither did Strickland, but they'd stood there for twenty minutes gawking at this painting of robed saints gathered on a celestial stage. It reminded Jackie of the mass growing up, how he'd inevitably tune out Father Nicoletti and scan the faces of martyrs painted along the ceiling, how Joey would sock him in the arm, how easy things felt between them then. In Marciano's fresco, Strickland pointed out a face in the swirling underbelly of cumulus. The painter had hidden something awful there, a face too ugly for language, scowling and horned like Satan himself, the same antichrist Cassavetes had glimpsed in *Rosemary's Baby*. They stared at this face for an uncomfortable length of time until at last Pietro Marciano appeared in the doorway, big as an ox, stogie on his lips, half-full bottle of Strega in his mitt. He pointed at Jackie and said, *"You made it,"* in Italian, and Jackie confirmed that he did. Marciano nodded, and Jackie Donato had no choice but to submit to the great man, to follow the neorealist wherever he planned to lead him.

• • •

Pietro Marciano's office featured long sloping windows that overlooked the grounds and palm trees, yoked by the rising sun. An elegant desk sat between them, littered with papers and tchotchkes, clutter Jackie would have expected from his family back home, not an international power broker, let alone the man who dreamed *La Penitenza* into reality. They both clutched glasses of Strega—for digestion, Marciano insisted—even though Jackie could barely see straight.

"So," Marciano started in English, "tell me where you're from?"

Jackie knew what this meant and put up a minor resistance. "New York."

Marciano waved his fist. "No, I mean your people."

"Sicily. A village in the center. They were sulfur miners."

"Bello." But from the flutter of Marciano's eyes, Jackie knew it wasn't *bello* at all, that every Roman he met asked where he was from and scoffed when he answered Sicily, a land—according to them—of medieval peasants ill-suited to modernity.

"I don't like small talk, so let's get to it." Marciano opened a drawer and retrieved two 16-millimeter reels. "I've seen *Are You There, Cugino?* and *Spiritual Pain*, and I like the way you carry yourself."

"How did you get your hands on those?"

"I'm Pietro Marciano." He shrugged, and Jackie couldn't deny there was something extraordinarily charismatic about him, but even that phrase didn't do the man justice. Jackie felt a tiny flame growing hot and steady behind his chest, animating his flesh in a way that made him extremely sensitive to the world. He wasn't starstruck, because Jackie hadn't felt this way while meeting so many of his heroes, not Cassavetes or even John Ford. In those moments, he felt shy and less than, doubting he could ever match those giants. In Marciano's villa on the outskirts of Rome, Jackie felt himself opening to a deeper truth, a reality where all dreams and nightmares were suddenly and violently possible.

"I knew from *Are You There, Cugino?* and *Spiritual Pain* that you had talent. But there are a lot of talented people who don't have the inner strength necessary to become a director in the truest sense of that word. That quality is rare, and I needed to meet you to learn if you have it or not."

He couldn't help himself. "Do I have it?"

Marciano took a long puff from his cigar, and Jackie was mesmerized by the jeweled embers. "May I tell you a story?"

The cold from the previous evening had passed, and Jackie felt his skin warming with the rising sun. "Of course."

"I got my start in 1936 when I was discovered after writing an essay about Fritz Lang's *M* in *Cinema*. Do you know who edited *Cinema*?"

"No."

Marciano laughed. "You Sicilians never know your history. Vittorio Mussolini edited *Cinema*. You've heard of his father, at least? Il Duce?"

Nothing about this moment felt real to Jackie, and yet it also seemed like the plateau he'd been crawling toward his entire life. "I know about Il Duce," he finally said.

"A lot of people don't know that Cinecittà was founded by Mussolini as a propaganda machine, that Il Duce's son loved film and dreamed of assembling his own army of directors who would create movies that inspired Italian fascists to historic greatness."

There was a stilted quality to Marciano's speech, and Jackie sensed this was a monologue the neorealist had delivered many times before, even in English.

"Vittorio admired my essay, and he invited me for coffee on the Via Veneto. How could I refuse? This was 1936 you must remember. The fascists had been in power for over a decade." Another puff of his cigar. "He offered me a job as an assistant director on a film Il Duce himself was producing, *Scipio Africanus,* about the Romans besting Hannibal in the third century. It was slop intended to manipulate support for our fascist misadventures in Africa." Marciano switched from English to Italian. *"What do you think I did?"* he asked. *"My father was a dedicated leftist, had organized socialist meetings, had been made to drink castor oil when the blackshirts came to power when I was still wearing short pants. What do you think I did?"*

Everything was quiet, and Jackie understood then that he'd been summoned to Rome primarily to answer a series of questions. This didn't intimidate him. On the contrary, Jackie felt as though somehow he'd always known the answer, that it was a crucial part of his identity, like his face or voice or all those hours surrendered to his mother's church. *"You took the job,"* Jackie replied in Italian.

"Of course I did. And I took another and another and another, assisting on five fascist films in total until the government came crashing down in '43, when we were occupied by the Nazis."

The Strega tasted bitter in Jackie's mouth. If everything Marciano told him was true, then it recast *La Penitenza,* a film about a reluctant fascist who seeks forgiveness and ultimately commits suicide as penance. Jackie had felt this way perhaps a dozen times in his life, moments when he drank so much that he sailed beyond drunkenness and landed on a new coast where he could finally see himself and the world so clearly. *"So Marcello,"* Jackie said, *"the protagonist of* La Penitenza, *that's you."*

"No. Marcello was not me," Marciano said with a great big laugh. *"Marcello was meant to represent a moral weakness I observed in those post-War years, mostly in artists who'd benefited from fascism and now, suddenly, had a change of heart and wanted to hang on the cross to prove how deeply they regretted their behavior. These people—directors, writers, painters, people from every artistic field who counted on fascism as their benefactor—burned out immediately, eaten alive by their guilt and self-loathing.* La Penitenza *did not celebrate them. It condemned*

them, each and every one." He let this settle. *"Jackie, I did not believe in fascism, and I do not subscribe to any political theory now present in the world. I'm an artist who exists outside of politics, and frankly I would have surrendered anything to become a director. Swearing my loyalty to the fascists was nothing compared to that desire. I would have given up so much more."*

Marciano refilled their glasses of Strega. *"When a layperson watches a film, they see what's onscreen, the moving images. When a director watches a film, we see behind the camera, the turbulent struggle of the artist. We know immediately if a director has it or not. I watched* Spiritual Pain *and knew immediately that we were simpatico, that you would cut ties with every human being you'd ever met to remain there behind the camera, out of view but in control. Tell me I'm wrong."*

At first, Jackie wanted to protest. He would not surrender to fascism just to make a movie, and he would not sacrifice his relationships with other human beings just to become a director. But then, the dark truth Marciano had been guiding him toward appeared fully formed. Of course he would. Of course. He would gladly cut ties with the lot of them—his mother and father, his brother, Strickland, Cassavetes, all the friends he made playing stickball back home, all those beautiful and intelligent people who invited him into their homes for endless lines of cocaine—to not only make *Spiritual Pain*, but any film no matter how insipid. And what haunted Jackie Donato for the rest of his life was how true this remained. Even on his deathbed, he knew he'd only met four people in his entire life he would have chosen over making a film—his third wife long dead, one of his six children, and two of his nine grandchildren. He would gladly erase everyone else if it meant even one more hour behind the camera, one more second arranging reality exactly in the correct order. Jackie accepted this painful truth and understood then why so many directors happily took counsel from Pietro Marciano. They were all the same.

"I want you to stay with me," Marciano said, taking his silence as confirmation. *"For the next month. Be my guest. Your producer too. I want to introduce you to some people, bring you to Cinecittà, then up north to meet the judges of the Venice Film Festival. I read Phoebe King's review, and she's completely wrong about you. You'll be one of my boys now. What do you say?"*

A spotted starling landed on the palm tree outside. Its cry sounded artificial to the directors, mechanical and not of this world, too powerful for its little bones, its minuscule ounces of flesh. Jackie sipped his Strega and said of course, thank you, he was thrilled. He never spoke to his brother again.

Her Final Nights

On my way to a first date, I found an unlabeled VHS sitting on the sidewalk. I paused, straightened my skirt, and tried to remember how long it had been since I'd seen one, that bulky cartridge that meant Disney or cheap cartoons when I was a child. I didn't mean to pick it up at first. I just wanted to touch it and remember that grainy plastic feel, the exterior of a dead world. But then I was holding it, and before I knew exactly how it happened, I tucked the tape into my purse and hurried along, hopeful that no one had seen. It felt like a good omen for a first date, and I fingered the new bulge in my purse as I entered the restaurant.

I'd chosen an Italian place in the trendy quarter of town, far from the low-class bars and strip clubs that had been erected, destroyed, and resurrected so many times as Fort McMurray boomed and burst and boomed again. I was on the older side for Tinder, a smidge above forty, and knew better than to let potential partners suggest a date, lest I end up at a chain restaurant. I found her at a table by the bar. Jenny Kwon. Twenty-five. I matched with men and women, and I'd long ago given up on trying to find partners exceedingly close to my own age. Twenty-something boys. Women in their fifties. I didn't care. We knew how close last call was, and it didn't make sense not to look for comfort wherever you might find it.

Jenny stood and pumped my hand, and I knew immediately from her cheap, colorful clothing that she had nothing to do with the tar sands.

"Angie Verrastro?" Jenny asked. "Great to meet you. The food here looks incredible. I'm so excited."

I peeled open the drink menu. "Have you been here before?" I asked knowingly.

"No way. I work a few blocks south from here, but I usually stick to Wolf Hollow, Quesada Libre, Modern Thai."

The trash places for the young. "Should we order a bottle of wine?"

Jenny tilted her head. "I'm more into bourbon."

"Bourbon it is."

We ordered drinks, and although it usually took me two or three stiff pours to feel even remotely tipsy, this one hit me fast. It was my first day off in nearly a week, and I tried to remember what exactly had led to this point. A quick trip to the gym. Maybe a bowl of ice cream for lunch? I'd barely eaten and knew immediately that I'd become drunk. Jenny's cheeks were already red, and I knew by the way she tore into the bread that she felt buzzed too. "Bread is so good, right?" she asked, her mouth full.

Before I could reply, my phone buzzed in my purse. I held it to my face, pretended to listen for ten seconds, and said I'd take care of it in the morning. When you go on as many first dates as I do, it's important to schedule escapes. I paid for a service that called me ten minutes into a date and then again at the hour mark. People don't like to hear this, but you know if you're going to sleep with them in the first ten minutes. Maybe they bring up their ex. Maybe they spend too much time talking about climate change. Ten minutes is all I need, and the second check in is just in case I change my mind, if my mood's soured and I'm suddenly craving a night alone in my apartment watching a documentary or messing around in VR. I looked at Jenny and felt certain we would sleep together. I'm sure we both wanted a momentary escape.

I ordered the foie gras tortellini while Jenny opted for the pasta negra with sea urchin chili and mussels, an adventurous choice for someone who stuck to the young part of town. Usually, when I brought twenty-somethings to my restaurants, they ordered classier versions of meals they already regularly ate. She handed the menu to the waiter and grinned. "So, what do you do exactly? What brought you to McMurray?"

I finished my drink and ordered a second. "I'm a chemist with Nalco Champion. Do you know Nalco?"

She shook her head.

"It's an ecolab that provides research and best practices for the oil companies extracting the tar sands. 'Drilling, cementing, fracturing, and stimulation,'" I quoted. "That's our motto."

She nodded, unsurprised and unimpressed. Almost everyone in Fort McMurray was either involved with the tar sands or worked in hospitality. She must have guessed from my clothes, my Gucci purse, the choice of restaurant, which side I was on and how much money I made. She ordered a second and asked if I liked my job.

"Of course not. Are you kidding? I absolutely hate it." Maybe the bourbon freed me up a bit, but this was how I'd felt for years, maybe ever since I moved here after finishing my PhD. I buttered a piece of bread and asked, "What about you? My job is so boring, Jenny. What do you do?"

She blushed and looked at her sneakers. "My job is so fucking stupid."

"Tell me."

"You know that new pizza place a few blocks from here? Strada Dada?"

It was on my list of restaurants to investigate. Upscale Neapolitan pizza helmed by a chef from Modena, one of the culinary capitals of Italy. My grandfather's people came from Modena or maybe it was Monza. I could never keep it straight. "I've been dying to try it."

"Well, it's really, really good. Like it's the best pizza I've ever eaten in my life. Not that I really know. I grew up in Victoria before it went underwater. Only pizza we had growing up was Pizza Pizza, and even as a kid I thought it tasted like cardboard. Our head chef at Strada Dada? She gets everything fresh, imported straight from Italy. She has connections to some exporter that has the last remaining stock of tomatoes from Naples from before it washed away. It's so fucking good."

"What do you do there? You cook?"

Jenny laughed. "No. They have this big brick oven, and the chef needs it to be so hot that the fire can never go out. If it goes out, it'd take days, maybe weeks to get back to the right temperature. So my job is to just come in at closing time and keep it going all night."

I stared at her. "You're kidding. You just keep the fire going?"

"I just keep the fire going."

"What does that even mean?"

"I prod the embers. If things get really spicy, I toss in a fresh block of wood. Mostly, I just read magazines or watch *Space Idol* on my phone. My body smells like smoke. Everything I own smells like smoke."

"Are you in charge of acquiring the wood?"

She shook her head. "Nah. Chef has another guy for that."

The waiter returned with our new drinks and Jenny quickly guzzled half. She was racing toward drunkenness, and that excited me. Alcohol was always the shortcut to getting to know someone, to making them comfortable enough to reveal the messy edges we all concealed on first dates. Time was melting away, and that's all I ever wanted from these encounters—a brief bubble where we temporarily escaped what was next. "So, you spend forty hours a week literally just watching a fire?"

"Yeah. Great way to spend my golden years, am I right? When everything comes crashing down, I can look back and say, 'Well, Jenny, you sure kept that fire raging for those rich oil fucks.' Oh, sorry, I didn't mean you. I didn't mean to imply you're a rich oil fuck."

I waved her off. If I wasn't a rich oil fuck, who was?

"Hey." Jenny leaned forward. "Let me ask you something. I always ask the tar sand people this on first dates. It's really important to me."

My body felt so warm. "Go on."

"How much time do you think we have left? Really. Don't sugarcoat it like you assholes do on the news."

This was the only thing people ever wanted to know—not how to stop it, but when it would end. "I can't give you an accurate estimate . . ."

Her face hardened.

"But," I said through a laugh, "my guess is ten years. Maybe twenty if we don't hit any drilling breakthroughs over the next five."

Jenny pointed her fork at me. "You pass the test."

"Yeah? How so?"

"You gave it to me straight. You're a realist just like me. I hate these oil people who claim we have fifty, a hundred years. Kill the earth. Don't kill the earth. I don't care. But be honest about it."

"You're the coolest pizza fire keeper I know, Jenny."

"Obviously."

• • •

I moved to Fort McMurray eight years ago with the same idea as everyone else—get rich off the tar sands and move to a beach within ten years. The problem is the beaches are moving. Miami, Hawaii, Barcelona, Cape Town, all gone, washed away. Oil people feared the government or UN would crack down, but they only deregulated us more, claimed they couldn't sink the global economy during a crisis. So in came the climate refugees to places like McMurray and Oklahoma and Alaska and Saudi Arabia and all the other fracking operations left standing. They sped up the process and created more sunken cities, more climate refugees. The work for laborers in McMurray is dangerous, but it's one of the last places on earth where the working-class can still get rich. Might as well enjoy our last decade or two before everything drowns.

Like most tar sand insiders, I worked seven days on, seven days off. That meant maintaining a "normal" relationship was pretty much impossible. Things started great—all that time together—but always cooled after a month of off-days not syncing up. That's why I resorted to Tinder and quick flings on my first day off that would hopefully extend throughout the week. Nobody wants to face the end alone, but I'm not too keen on limiting my choice of dance partners if I'm going to die at fifty. I date and fuck and ghost and repeat the process over and over again like everybody else in

McMurray, like everybody else everywhere else. Jenny Kwon could make me forget the world just as well as Hector Boyle or Jane Amador or Doug Hampton or any of my other recent dates. I just needed a body.

My phone went off at the hour mark. I reached in my purse and brushed the VHS I'd grabbed from the street earlier. I'd forgotten about it and kind of wanted to share this strange discovery with Jenny. Instead, I pressed the Do Not Disturb button and came clean.

"No one's really calling me. It's just a service I use to get out of dates if they're going badly."

Jenny laughed. "You serious? That's fucking great. You have to give me their website or something. I'd pay for that."

We were drunk, and the restaurant felt like it had disappeared. It was just me and Jenny, and the small portions of pasta weren't doing anything to sop up the alcohol in our bodies. In this new world, we opened up to each other in an artificial way I knew we wouldn't have otherwise.

"My older brother died when I was thirteen," Jenny said dramatically. "Motorcycle accident. Took his bike on the ferry to Seattle and died on some highway. I don't even know why he was there. It felt like such a huge tragedy at the time. But now it's like, hello, everybody's going to die anyway. You wasted all those tears and all that therapy, dummy."

I decided to be brave and reached out and held Jenny's hand. "I know exactly what you mean. Every woman in my family died of breast cancer. We weren't well-off financially. It was difficult, and they all suffered. I spent so many years terrified I'd die the same way, that the cancer was already inside of me, and now it doesn't even matter."

"I wanted to be a professor," Jenny said. "I wanted to teach Victorian novels."

"Victorian novels! Why?"

"They gave me a fantasy world I could live inside of for hours, days, weeks. I wanted to show that to others. I'm ready to apply to grad school, but it'll take seven years minimum. Why even fucking bother?"

"So, you're saying you're better off watching a fire in Strada Dada?"

Jenny raised her glass. "Hell yeah. Better to watch it burn than be burnt up. 'Better to get drunk, high, laid, paid if this is really the end.' You know that song? Lady Gaga's third act is fucking banging."

"I loved her when I was a child." Jenny made me feel like the first day of sunshine after months of cold and snow. Remember this? What life used to be like? She looked into my eyes and really made me believe I could fix everything, even if I knew that was a lie, that by morning I'd compile her imperfections, counting down the days until I returned to work and never saw her again.

"The way I see it," Jenny said, "is I have to experience all the happiness, all the excitement, all the joy I would have felt over the next fifty years in the next five. That means fuck impulse control and fuck plans." She dug around in her purse and showed me the orange flash of a prescription bottle. "Do you want to go back to my place and snort Adderall?"

I hadn't been asked to snort Adderall since college, when I was that dorky working-class girl from Uranium City trying desperately to fit in at the University of Saskatchewan, which might as well have been Toronto or Manhattan, might as well have been Mars. "OK," I said. "OK."

• • •

Normally, I would never have agreed to go back to someone's apartment if they worked in hospitality and not the tar sands. Jenny Kwon lived in the shit part of McMurray, miles from the luxury apartments among rows and rows of cheap, brick tenements put up in a hurry when the first wave of climate refugees swarmed Canada. Her apartment felt like time travel, like she'd guided me back to my social life in grad school. Postcards of distant—and now sunken—cities taped to the walls. Gaudy Christmas lights still blinking in February. Ironic furniture lifted from thrift stores and even a genuine record player. I watched her locate Lady Gaga's *The Fame* in a milk crate and set the needle in the groove.

"*The Fame*! You probably weren't even alive when this came out."

Jenny grabbed a mortar and pestle off the shelf and unscrewed her prescription bottle. She joined me on the couch and put her hand on my thigh. "I like old things."

I wanted to sigh in her face. I knew she thought of me that way—old—but it was such a turnoff to actually hear it, even if she was trying to shape those feelings into something sexy, something that proved her desire. I wanted to tell her that I felt permanently twenty-eight, that I doubted I'd learned anything or changed even remotely over the last decade plus, that in many ways, she felt more like a peer to me than my actual peers. Did everyone feel this way? Or was this just how people felt at the end? A permanent adolescence meant to keep doomsday at bay? I didn't know and couldn't explain any of this to Jenny, drunk as we were. So, I watched her crush up pills and reassemble them into two neat lines on the album cover. There was Lady Gaga wearing oversized sunglasses, blissfully unaware of the future. Jenny rolled up a dollar bill and said, "Bottoms up."

Snorting Adderall always made me euphoric, and within minutes, my mouth was dry and all negative feelings about Jenny washed away. What did they matter? We would be dead soon, and here was this warm, flesh-and-blood human willing to spend one of her final nights with me. This was inherently good, and I wanted so badly to believe that. We danced to Gaga, and this was all foreplay, all love, all resistance against the end, and when "Poker Face" came on, I shouted, "I danced to this in kindergarten!" and sang along to every single word until Jenny kissed me hard on the mouth during the first chorus. She really did smell like smoke.

"I fucking love you!" she lied.

"I love you too!" I lied back.

• • •

I'd experienced the kind of sex I had with Jenny before, increasingly so as we drifted toward the end. It was sweet and full of false promises—the I-love-you's, and I'll-marry-you's, and the you're-the-best-thing-that's-ever-happened-to-me-honey even though we'd only just met. We wanted to briefly understand what marriage felt like, what true intimacy felt like, similar to how I'd linger in parks and watch the dwindling number of children funnel down slides or fly through swings. What would it feel like to raise one? I'd never know, and I had to make peace with that.

When we finished, Jenny and I tugged on our underwear and returned to the couch. She played a contemporary record I didn't recognize that made me feel old. Our euphoria died as did any idea that this night had been meaningful in the way we'd hoped for an hour earlier. We passed a PBR back and forth in silence, and I was desperate to find anything to kill time, to make the clock run faster until it would be acceptable to slip out or suggest we sleep—I still didn't know if I wanted Jenny again in the morning or if I should try another Tinder date the next evening. And that's when I remembered the VHS.

"Hey," I said, face bright again, "you're never going to believe what happened on the way to the restaurant."

"What's that?" Jenny picked at her cuticles and looked disinterested, like she'd ordered something adventurous and was deeply unhappy with the results.

I lifted my purse from the floor and showed her the VHS. "Do you even know what this is?"

Jenny swiped it, excited again. "Of course I know what this is. I love these. How kitsch."

"It was just sitting there on the street. Can you believe it? What's a tape doing on the street decades after being replaced? I wish we could watch it."

Jenny flashed me the same grin from when she suggested Adderall. "Guess what, bitch?"

"What?"

She stood up. "I have a motherfucking VCR."

"What?"

She winked. "That's right. Have it in a box of my parents' stuff I never got rid of. They had the right cables to make it work on new TVs too. I tested it. But they only had *Weekend at Bernie's II*. Funny flick though."

Jenny disappeared into the bedroom and reappeared a moment later with a cardboard box labeled PARENTS. She hadn't mentioned them, and I wondered what happened, if their story was any different from the mundane tragedy I imagined in my head. She set the box down and dug out the dull gray machine I remembered from childhood, the one we clung to long after they went out of fashion.

"Are we sure we should do this?" I asked, suddenly afraid.

She crawled behind the TV and plugged in the wires. "Why not? You think it's a home movie? Maybe a sex tape? What did they call those videos where people actually died?"

"Snuff films."

"Yeah. Wouldn't that be awesome?"

Jenny emerged from behind the TV and fed the tape into the VCR. She returned to the couch with the old remote and asked if I was ready. She held my hand, and her body looked so young, so healthy, and I could barely believe she'd be ash in just a few short years.

"I'm ready."

She pressed play. Static flashed across the screen. We leaned closer and closer, waiting for anything.

The Electric City

Angelo knew there was trouble from the frantic gait of Franny's walk, how she shoved open the glass doors of the Ritz and scanned the lobby not with familiarity, but with panic. She locked eyes with him manning the concession stand in his red bowtie and marched in his direction, her flats squeaking across the polished floors. Little Jimmy made for the register, but Angelo told him, "I got it." They'd already started the late show on both screens—*Jaws 2* and *Capricorn One*—and the Ritz was dead even for a Thursday night. *Hooper* one-sheets hung throughout the lobby, and Angelo felt watched by Burt Reynolds, his oversized pupils drilling into him.

"Angelo." Franny set her enormous black purse on the counter. "It's Frankie. He's in trouble."

Angelo told Little Jimmy to go mop the bathrooms. Then he retrieved his toothpick from behind his ear and set it over his lower lip, between two chalky molars. He'd been best friends with Frankie and Franny ever since they were kids, had marched up the aisle of St. Anthony's with them to receive their first holy communions. They were twenty-three years old now, and most of their friends had long ago retreated into backbreaking jobs at Tobyhanna or Scranton Lace. Franny served up soda pop at Abe's Jewish round the corner. Frankie ran the numbers. Angelo worked here.

"What happened?" he asked.

"He won't tell me exactly, but he says it's bad, real bad. He's holed up at the Silver Trolley. Refuses to see me. Says he needs to see you. I think it's . . ." She paused and glanced around to make sure Little Jimmy was gone. "I think it's you-know-who."

Angelo opened the popcorn machine and grabbed a handful of perfectly popped kernels—he'd long ago perfected how to chew popcorn in one side of his mouth while maintaining his toothpick in the other. He hadn't seen Frankie since last Sunday, when they bumped into each other at Whiskey Dick's and watched the Phils surrender four runs to Atlanta. One thing led to another, and Angelo almost had to call out of work the next afternoon.

"You-know-who," he repeated. "So what? He wants me to come see him after work?"

Franny shook her head, and again Angelo's eyes drifted to the *Hooper* one-sheet and its smirking Burt Reynolds watching them from some great beyond. "No. I just talked with him. He needs to see you now. Right now."

It was a quarter to ten. The Silver Trolley was on the other side of downtown, near the Lackawanna River and the bus station. If Angelo timed it right, he could be back in time to chase the winos out during the credits of *Capricorn One*.

Angelo placed his hand over Franny's and looked into her red eyes, the pupils of someone who had obviously been crying. He remembered in eighth grade how they danced together at the year-end celebration, a rinky-dink affair in the auditorium of a nunnery, how Sister Lucy shoved a ruler between their bodies and shouted, "Leave space for the Holy Ghost!" He squeezed her hand now and said, "Don't worry. I'll help him."

• • •

The Silver Trolley was the kind of dump you rented by the hour, a fleabag high-rise that had been a tenement a hundred years earlier when Italians and Irish and Polish flocked en masse to Scranton looking for work in the rich vein of anthracite that had all but dried up by the time Angelo was born. He'd never entered the Silver Trolley before, but walked in with as much faux confidence as he could muster. The inside was a narrow alcove, staircase on your left, a little office behind bulletproof glass on your right. Angelo rang the bell and noted the dirty glass, all those fingerprints, how different it looked from the snack counter at the Ritz, how Mr. Sabato would turn red faced if Little Jimmy forgot to wipe it down every other hour.

A shirtless goon wandered into frame, his drawers held up by threadbare suspenders. He looked more like clay than a human being, and the folds around his bald head reminded Angelo of Frankie's long-dead pug, Dominic, a dog they played with along the spoil tips of coal in the woods.

The man who looked like Dominic chomped the end of his stogie. "Yeah?"

Angelo choked down his humiliation and gave the fake name Franny had insisted on. "I'm looking for Deano Sinatra."

Dominic gave him the side eye. "So?"

Angelo slid a Lincoln through the gap of the bulletproof glass.

"Room 307."

He climbed three flights of stairs, rolling his sleeves as he did so. It was June, and the first rash of summer heat had settled into the valley, shocking Angelo like it did every year, sweat pooling at the small of his back and under his armpits. He heard muffled TVs and moaning through the paper-thin walls, and Angelo felt grateful that he'd left his bow tie and paper hat at the Ritz, a completely different world.

At Room 307 he knocked once, twice, waited five seconds, then knocked again—just like Franny instructed. The cheap door didn't budge, but he heard Frankie's voice on the other side. "Who's it?" he barked in a too deep baritone, a put-on if he'd ever heard one.

"You made me leave work, now let me in," Angelo shouted back.

The door cracked open revealing a sweltering room lit by the blinking neon of the nearby bus station. Three empty boxes of Buona Pizza on the gummy carpet. Two nearly empty bottles of Jack lined up like little soldiers on the nightstand. And then of course Frankie himself in white underwear and undershirt, sweat-stained, his dark hair matted to his face. So different from how he usually presented in leather jacket, hair slicked back, smelling of cologne, a playful smile on his lips. Frankie was always the beautiful one, the prettiest of their trio, the smoothest, and it was this contrast with lanky Franny—everybody's little sister—that transformed them from two separate people into the legendary "Frankie and Franny." Angelo remembered exactly when his friends became a couple, after the three of them saw *Paint Your Wagon* in ninth grade and the antics of Lee Marvin and Clint Eastwood excited Frankie so much that he kissed Franny right on the lips as the credits rolled. His two friends had been on-again, off-again ever since, and although Frankie cheated on her occasionally, Franny remained true, singing the many praises of the beautiful boy from the east side who deep down was the sweetest guy this side of Appalachia. They were one of *those* couples, famous throughout the valley.

Frankie grabbed Angelo by the collar and yanked him inside the motel room, resetting the deadbolt in one practiced motion. "I knew I could count on you, ol' buddy." He gestured to the bed like he'd been hosting people there for years. "Sit down. Get comfy. Let me make you something."

He grabbed the Jack and two Styrofoam cups from Buona, but Angelo waved him off. "Don't. You know I'm assistant manager now. I should get back before the late show lets out."

Frankie poured two huge drinks anyway. "We're not finishing before the late show. Here. Salute."

Angelo drank a small sip of the whiskey—just enough to be polite—and watched Frankie swallow his in one long gulp. "You look like shit," he told him.

"Thanks, pal." He sat next to Angelo on the bed, reeking of alcohol and sweat. He looked like he actually might cry, something Angelo hadn't seen him do since Dominic got loose and was run over by a Buick when they were kids.

"Mind explaining what the hell's going on?"

Frankie refilled his drink. "I maybe owe a substantial sum of money."

Angelo reinserted his toothpick and stared up at the ceiling. There was a brown water stain in the far-left corner that kind of looked like Paul Newman if you squinted right. If Frankie owed the bookies less than two hundred bucks—a common occurrence during baseball season—then he could still get back in time to close the Ritz with Little Jimmy. "How much?"

"50k."

Angelo stood up and mindlessly drifted closer to the Paul Newman water stain. Fifty thousand was completely unfathomable, more money than either of their fathers—former coal miners reduced to schlubs manning cash registers like all the other old timers—had ever seen in their lives. Angelo hid a stogie box under his bed where he kept all his savings from the Ritz. Six years of mopping floors, passing out tickets, sweeping his flashlight over young couples fondling each other while Roger Moore foiled the villains time and again had amounted to a little under two grand. When he started squirreling away money as a teenager, Angelo told himself he was saving up to move to Philly, Pittsburgh, maybe even New York City or California. But now, he didn't know what purpose the old stogie box served. Every day was a rerun of the day before, and he had no idea how to break the cycle or even if he still wanted to. He was the second Delrosso born in the valley, and he felt a kind of gravity tethering him to its streets, this soil, the Ritz.

"How could you possibly owe 50k?"

This was purely rhetorical because Angelo already understood. After high school, Frankie fell in with the bookies, the wannabe toughs who considered themselves mobsters even though they'd never as much robbed a gas station. But Angelo knew that Frankie ran the numbers, an unofficial lotto steered by what passed for the local mob. Angelo had even gone with Frankie a few times, traveling from storefront to storefront downtown, recording people's guesses, collecting their cash. And these trips never ended without a celebratory drink at Classico where Frankie would sidle up next to Joe the Bookie and place enormous bets using other people's money on the Phils, the Steelers, once even a JV volleyball squad. But Frankie just winked at Angelo whenever he lost. No need to worry because he always had a backup plan. Just go double or nothing to get whole. And if that failed, go double or nothing again and again until you finally broke even. With that strategy, it was only a matter of time before he racked up some outrageous debt that would cause even the good-natured Joe the Bookie to balk.

"What are you gonna do?" Angelo asked.

Frankie lay on the bed and crossed his boots. "I need to leave town."

"Come on." Neither of them had ever left for more than two or three nights at the Jersey shore—Ocean City as kids, Atlantic City much later. "You think these guys are gonna kill you or something? This isn't Philly."

"I heard they got guys waiting for me at the bus station and Avoca. My old man said a Caddy's been parked outside our house for two days. Franny's too." He opened the nightstand and slowly, ever so slowly, showed Angelo a gun, holding it above his head like the priest with the Eucharist in church. Gleaming steel. Outside of the movies, Angelo had never seen a gun in his life and watched helplessly as Frankie balanced it over his wrist and pointed in his direction.

"Are you crazy?" He moved away from the gun and opened the window. Downtown was dead aside from the lit-up bars. Neither of them owned a car, and they couldn't just walk out of Scranton. It was bumblefuck in every direction. "So you're just gonna bail on Franny?" he asked.

The only sounds came through the open window, the whooshing of cars and trucks along the newly built highway connecting Scranton to Wilkes-Barre, Hazelton, Harrisburg, Altoona, and the many places beyond. Frankie hid the gun in his waistband.

"She's better off without me."

"You have a plan then?" Angelo asked.

"Sure, but I need your help."

• • •

No one could agree on the exact boundaries of downtown, but Angelo figured it was the five-block stretch running from Lackawanna Avenue to the hills along Vine Street. This modest collection of buildings and streets contained so much of his young life. From the marquee of the Ritz to the courthouse in the center, downtown was crisscrossed by bars and pizza places, boarded-up buildings and abandoned storefronts. Overlooking everything was the dead neon sign which once blinked out THE ELECTRIC CITY in their grandparents' heyday, before the mines dried up, when Scranton housed the first electric trolley system in America. That sign malfunctioned two decades earlier, and still no one had fixed it. Angelo stared at it now, Frankie close by in a leather jacket with the collar pulled up, Italian horn dangling above his chest, looking every which way for any sign of danger, gun hidden behind his back.

They entered Whiskey Dick's, the kind of hole-in-the-wall bar frequented by beer-and-shot regulars all over the valley. No sign out front. A long rectangular bar occupied by a half dozen middle-aged men in Carhartts and shitkickers, a pile of dollars and coins in front of each of them, a dented Wurlitzer in back between two broken slots and a Winston cigarette machine. Angelo nodded at the bartender, a clever girl they went to school with. Gloria. Played the lead in *Hello, Dolly!* senior year and signed every yearbook with a kiss and "CYA IN NEW YORK CITY!" written in big floppy cursive. Frankie hung back as Angelo ponied up for two drafts of lager, the both of them scanning the room for marks. Angelo handed Frankie his beer and knew they didn't even have to discuss the target, that they both selected 'Cuso the Wop the second they saw him.

'Cuso the Wop sat in back by one of the wooden pillars, a draft in front of him along with his customary tin bucket with "IA2I" painted down the side in neat, childlike print. Frankie wandered over first, sitting two stools down, while Angelo hovered nearby, pretending to study the dart board. Two winters past, he'd waltzed in from the snow with Frankie and Franny after dragging them all to see *Rocky* at the Ritz. Franny rarely accompanied them to bars and preferred the kind of red checkered tablecloth joints she'd enjoyed as a kid—Arcaro's, Colarusso's, Cooper's,—and had only come because she'd been so moved by the many struggles of Sylvester Stallone. Her older brother installed a dart board in Franny's basement years earlier, and Angelo watched with delight as she decimated the disbelieving crowd of drunks at Whiskey Dick's, landing bullseye after bullseye until the men were laying bets and coughing up ten or even twenty bones a game.

Franny never cleaned her glasses—they contained as many fingerprints as the clerk's bulletproof partition at the Silver Trolley—and she always struck Angelo as a little lanky and kind of nerdy. That her hands possessed that level of grace and coordination affected him deeply.

"Hey, 'Cus," Frankie said all friendly. "How's the collection coming?"

'Cuso picked up his bucket and shook it, jingling the coins inside musically. Angelo knew from his rosy cheeks and mellow expression that 'Cuso was already drunk and felt a terrible guilt deep down in his stomach, like cussing as a child in those precious hours after holy confession. Angelo had known 'Cuso the Wop his whole life. Just about everyone in Scranton did from the way he drove up and down those hilly streets in his enormous jalopy of a Chrysler, how he'd park near busy corners and rattle his bucket and collect change, how he only gave it up late at night when he settled in for a long drink at Whiskey Dick's or the Glass Onion. Angelo's father claimed he hadn't always been like this, that he'd actually been a reliable halfback for the Dunmore Bucks maybe fifteen years earlier, but then he went to Vietnam and returned obsessed with his collection. "Hamburger Hill," Angelo's father confided over a pitcher at Jenny's Inn, and Angelo nodded like he had any idea what that meant. Angelo had only missed the draft by a few months and was extremely cognizant of that fact.

Frankie peeked inside 'Cuso the Wop's bucket. "Damn, that's a lot of scratch."

"You boys feel like donating?" 'Cuso sniffed before running a black plastic comb through his long dark hair. He was never unkempt and always wore flannel shirts and corduroy pants no matter the weather, a bulge in his chest pocket revealing just a slice from a box of smokes.

Frankie glanced over at Angelo and said, "Hmm. How about we donate to the cause, then share a little Jack?"

"Who's buying?" 'Cuso the Wop narrowed his eyes.

"I think Angelo here can cover us, isn't that right?" Frankie dropped some coins and a dollar bill into 'Cuso's bucket.

Angelo chewed his toothpick and said, "Fine." *Jaws 2* was about to let out, and he found himself missing all those tiny rituals, the moment when the Ritz emptied and finally became his. He glanced at smiling Frankie and couldn't reconcile that this was really his life, that Angelo's adult form had somehow emerged from that ancient boy obsessed with movies, that this Frankie was in any way connected to the child who played baseball on the playground, that even this incarnation of 'Cuso had sprung from a boy stomping puddles in this here valley. What, if anything, connected any of them beyond habit and inertia, a calcification meant to stand in for the childish bonds that had all but slipped away? And how much longer would this dull facsimile continue? How long would he wake up, make the coffee, eat breakfast, open the Ritz, close the Ritz? He felt in that moment like something had malfunctioned in his body, like he was a record skipping for all time, comfortable in its broken groove.

Frankie moved a stool closer to 'Cuso and ordered them all shots. Then he asked if 'Cus could explain the purpose behind his collection one more time.

"Sure," 'Cuso said, turning the bucket so the "IA2I" more properly faced them. "This here stands for 'Italian Americans 2 Italy.' Look, I'm sure I'm only telling you what you already know. We don't belong here, boys. None of us. Our parents and grandparents only left Italy to come here for work. But what happened? The mines went and dried up. What do you do, kid? For a living, I mean?"

"I run numbers."

'Cuso pointed at Angelo. "And you, kid?"

Angelo collected the three stiff pours of Jack on the rocks. "I'm over at the Ritz."

"Bullshit." 'Cuso the Wop spat on the ground. "Those are bullshit jobs. We don't belong here."

"So what's the collection for then?" Frankie asked.

They'd heard it all before, had listened to 'Cuso's spiel while shooting pool at Stalter's, while walking to the Convenient for smokes and Turkey Hill, while leaving high school and trying to sneak past him to their cars. Everyone in town knew the purpose of the bucket.

"This here," 'Cuso said, "is a collection to repatriate every last Italian American back to Italy. We're finally going home."

"How much more do you need?" Frankie asked.

A wino in an Eagles cap creased down the middle shambled to the jukebox. He fed in a dime, and the mechanical hand lifted a 45 and brought it to the center of the machine. A moment later, "Hey, Western Union Man" by Jerry Butler warbled out, his syrupy voice raising the dead bar back to life.

'Cuso scratched his chin. "Don't worry about the money, kid. Don't you worry about that one bit. I'd say we're about 90 percent of the way there. This time next summer you'll be kicking up beachside in Palermo, and everyone will call you signore. We'll be kings."

Frankie held up his glass. "Cheers to that."

'Cuso raised his in kind. "A hundred years."

• • •

Before long, 'Cuso the Wop was cataclysmically drunk, holding the bar for support, swaying ever so slightly like a wobbly bowling pin. Whiskey Dick's had emptied out this close to last call on a Thursday, and Frankie insisted that 'Cuso couldn't drive himself home, that it was their responsibility to return him safely to his doorstep. But 'Cuso told them, no, no, he could definitively prove that he wasn't drunk, that he was as sober as "a babe before holy baptism," and they watched as he rose from his stool and entered the semi-enclosed phonebooth in back, how he whispered into the receiver something soft and beautiful like a prayer. When he returned, he explained he'd just ordered an omelet from the Glider Diner, that it would be waiting for him in no time flat, that purchasing eggs and bacon and toast proved he wasn't drunk. Gloria the bartender flipped on the house lights and snapped her fingers at 'Cuso the Wop. "You're shitfaced, 'Cus. Let these nice boys drive you home. I know them. We went to school together. They won't hurt you."

Outside, Angelo and Frankie followed 'Cuso the Wop round the corner where he'd parked his rusted beige Chrysler in the handicapped spot by St.

Luke's. The windshield was covered with salmon parking tickets, and 'Cuso just brushed them off like snow after a beautiful dusting. The Ritz stood down the block, and Angelo stared at its dimmed marquee. Without that neon, the entire downtown felt dead, a foggy graveyard where any manner of evil might thrive. "Come on, 'Cus," Frankie said, getting closer to him now. "Listen to Gloria and hand over the keys."

Angelo watched his best friend reach around his back to the gun hidden under his jacket in the waistband of his jeans. The jacket rode up on his back, and his fingers snaked over the handle, gripping it now, pulling it ever so slightly from its hiding place. A gust of wind howled down the avenue, and then, miraculously, 'Cuso the Wop cursed and handed Frankie a rabbit foot attached to his dangling car keys. "Just remember this when we return to Italy," he said. "You both owe me an amaro. You'll call me signore!"

They laid 'Cuso across the backseat and listened to his mumbled directions, driving out of Scranton up into the lid of the valley where 'Cuso lived in a nice-looking duplex across from a playground with a basketball court. Angelo walked 'Cuso to his door, whispering, "We'll park the car in back for you, OK? I'll leave it in back."

When he returned, Frankie was all smiles, pounding the shredding interior roof of the Chrysler with his fist. "We fucking did it, pal. I told ya we could do it."

"Yeah, sure," Angelo said, staring out the window at the playground. "So now I drop you off at the bus station in Wilkes-Barre and bring the car back here?"

Frankie squeezed the steering wheel and studied the tiny neighborhood, the lone streetlight swaying in the summer wind, blinking an SOS to no one. "You mind indulging me first?"

• • •

Weiner Shack 2 sat a few miles east of 'Cuso the Wop's, up Route 6 by the state game lands in a lot that overlooked downtown, swaddled low in the valley by the twisting Lackawanna River on one side and train tracks on the other. They used to come here all the time in high school, would hitch a ride with some senior and eat chili dogs and french fries out of paper bags all night long. It wasn't the food that made Weiner Shack 2 such a hit, but that it stayed open all night and afforded such an incredible view. Angelo and Frankie sat in the empty parking lot now, sharing fries like in the old days, staring into the heart of the city that had raised them. From there, they could make out all the individual lights of the houses, all those sorry souls still awake, and Angelo thought it resembled a tapestry of stars, like the cosmos brought low to earth. Frankie had explained that Angelo would never see him again, but he didn't really believe it and was surprised by how he felt. He wasn't sad, because even that required you to still care. All Angelo felt was numb, a hollowed-out nothing where something important was supposed to sit. He remembered coming here a few weeks before graduation, how Angelo and Frankie had wasted an hour describing all the adult adventures they would surely now go on, how Angelo would learn the movie business in Hollywood and Frankie would travel east, maybe New York or Boston, saying he'd always wanted to wear a peacoat and work on the docks. When they asked Franny where she wanted to go, she turned very quiet and pushed her glasses up the ridge of her nose. "Nowhere," she told them, sounding surprised and even a little hurt that they had to ask. "I'm not a child anymore. I gave all that thinking up." She wrapped her arms around herself. "This is my home."

Angelo turned to Frankie now as they finished their fries and tossed the waste down into the valley. "There's no fifty-thousand-dollar debt, is there?"

"You figured it out, huh?" He lay back against the dirty windshield of 'Cuso's Chrysler. "Even I'm not fucking dumb enough to rack up 50k of gambling debt."

The wind howled. "So Franny's pregnant then?"

Frankie stared into the heavens, while Angelo looked down into the bowl of the valley. "Yeah," he finally admitted.

"You needed all this to look real so I wouldn't figure it out and tell her the truth?"

"Yeah," he repeated. "And I wanted to see you one last time."

Angelo didn't turn to look at him and instead located the Big Dipper in the night sky, just like his mother showed him when he was still a child, when the world felt large and impossible and free. He didn't realize then that's as big as it would ever get, that each year it would shrink smaller and smaller until the scope of his life was reduced to an ever-narrowing strip of land, nowhere to go but the miles of empty coal mines coiled beneath his feet. "Go back to Franny," he told his friend.

"I can't be a father, man. I can't."

They listened to two more songs on the radio until "Sing" by the Carpenters came on. This, Angelo thought, was particularly cruel. He hated that stupid song and how constantly it played five years ago, when they finished high school and all those banal rituals—graduation mass, prom, parties—as Karen Carpenter's upbeat voice commanded them to "sing of good things not bad / sing of happy not sad" while meanwhile he felt adrift and paralyzed. Karen Carpenter, he thought. Karen Carpenter.

Angelo hopped off the Chrysler and reached through the driver's side window to kill the radio. "We better get moving," he said.

Frankie swung his legs over the hood and stared at his friend. "You promise you won't tell her?"

Angelo put the key into the ignition and turned, the engine stuttering to life, the headlights erasing the valley below. "I promise." Then he drove Frankie to the bus station in Wilkes-Barre, and they never saw each other again.

The Complete Oral History of Monkey High School

Chapter 27: Li'l Einstein's Final Fate

Gina Sorrentino, Writer: After the holiday break in '87, the network informed us we only had four episodes to wrap up the show. I wasn't surprised. My agent had been hinting about it for weeks, and after the head writer jumped networks for *Night Court* and Ed Sheridan left Hollywood to grow mushrooms in Idaho, I knew the jig was up. The network never replaced them, so it was just me and Clark Francis in the writing room, and he was a fossil even back then. He'd burned himself out writing *Update* on the first season of *SNL* and would pitch a few lines to the group maybe two, three times each week. I had no clue how we were going to end the show with only the two of us, but it was obvious I was in charge. I was thirty years old and felt like I'd accomplished nothing. It was my final shot in Hollywood.

Benjamin Whitmore III, Former Network President: There's no conspiracy, all right? I've read these bloggers who try and claim I had some vendetta against Mr. Buttons, the monkey who played Li'l Einstein on *Monkey High School*. That's just not true, all right? I have a long record of being pro-monkey. I love putting animals in shows, just love it. I greenlit *Monkey*

High School, Donkey Hospital, even *Oink Oink's Playhouse*. The ratings just weren't there. The show pulled a decent share in the first season when the original showrunners stuck to the tried-and-true formulas, what we in the business call the T and T's. Your bully episodes, your befriending a nerd episodes, your first crush episodes. But when those veterans abandoned ship, the season two folks crawled up their own assholes with obscure political agendas. It was a show about a super intelligent monkey who goes to high school. We didn't need commentary on the Iran-Contra affair. But Christ, if we only knew what Sorrentino would pull in those final four episodes. In hindsight, the Iran-Contra episode gets lumped in with the good old days.

Gina Sorrentino, Writer: The whole reason I moved to Hollywood is I wanted to tell this personal story about leukemia. I had this best friend growing up in Rochester: Maria Aiello. We were inseparable, and people told us we looked like twins enough that it kind of sunk in. We both did ballet and poetry camp. We were both extroverts. Our parents bought us these huge stockpiles of sparklers each July, and we'd use them all year. We'd hold them above our heads and pump our bikes through the neighborhood. I started thinking about us as a unit, more like clones than twins. We lost touch during college, but we both ended up in Boston after graduation. I was working on an advanced degree, and Maria was bartending at this hole-in-the-wall, the Sweetwater Tavern. I still go there whenever I visit Boston which isn't too often these days, but anyway, I'm getting sidetracked. I'm kind of nervous. I've never told this story to the press before, but it was thirty years ago so what the hell? In Boston, Maria came down with the flu, or at least what she thought was the flu, but she didn't kick it. She did some blood work, and surprise, leukemia! Twenty-three years old, and she had leukemia.

Clark Francis, Writer: Did I know our leukemia arc was based in reality? Look. If we're being honest here about the whole *Monkey High School* fiasco, it wasn't exactly a bright period for me. I was still kind of reeling from Belushi's death, and I thought maybe Sorrentino's leukemia episodes drew some inspiration from Gilda's diagnosis a year or two earlier. I don't know. I was fifteen years older than Sorrentino. We didn't run in the same circles. She wasn't into my lifestyle. Do you see what I'm saying? Look. Once I did a line off Mr. Buttons' butt cheeks. It was a dark time. Praise above I eventually found the Quakers.

Gina Sorrentino, Writer: Now you're probably expecting me to tell you I was the perfect best friend and by Maria's side for her entire illness. But that's not true. I avoided her. Sure, I visited her in the hospital a few times. We went out for steaks once, and near the end we even met up at the Cineplex—it was *The King of Comedy*, a movie I still can't bring myself to rewatch—and I remember that Maria had to wear these paper slippers over her shoes and this mask over her mouth, and after we said goodbye, I cried all the way home on the Green Line. So, eventually Maria dies, and I endure this long introspective period. I'm talking like three weeks where I keep imagining what it would be like if I'd been diagnosed instead of Maria, instead of my clone. I didn't even go to her funeral in Rochester and made some excuse that I was too busy with classes, but really I was probably just drinking Shiraz and thinking vaguely romantic thoughts in my studio. So after these three weeks, I realize how selfish I've been. How I never really grieved for Maria or even thought about her suffering. It was an odd realization, to understand firsthand how selfish you could be, how easily you could leave someone behind you've known your entire life. I wrote a screenplay about it, and that's what landed me an agent, and that's what led me to Hollywood. I moved at twenty-five and felt so stupidly confident in my own abilities that I assumed my screenplay would be optioned within the first three months. It never happened. I jumped from one fledgling sitcom to the next, and by the time I was writing for *Monkey High School*, I was thirty and thinking pretty heavily about moving back East. If I didn't tell my story right then it was never going to happen.

Felix Brown, Animal Handler: I am not a fan of those final four episodes, no sir. Neither was Mr. Buttons. We hated them because Gina Sorrentino, this self-obsessed east coaster who thought she'd landed herself on a serious drama, shifted the focus away from Mr. Buttons' character Li'l Einstein and put it on the two kids: Riley and Melissa. Remind me. What's the name of the show? Oh, that's right. It's *Monkey High School*. Not *Human High School*. *Monkey High School*. If the monkey's not front and center, then what are we even doing?

Chaz Eagleton, Agent: Yeah, I remember where I was when Sorrentino called and said she wanted to use her leukemia script for the final four episodes of *Monkey Whatever*: downing oysters with Emilio and Andrew at Spago. We were hammering out this project with a cokehead executive from Paramount that never materialized. It truly would've been tremendous. Emilio and Andrew as turn-of-the-century farmers who inherit their father's land only to see their simple lives devastated by industrialization. It was a metaphor for what happened to Emilio and Andrew after they got big, and it would've been something all right. Would've altered the trajectories of their careers, you can count on that. Hard to imagine *Weekend at Bernie's II* or *Mighty Ducks* if that farming picture got made. What I'm trying to say is that Gina Sorrentino wasn't exactly a priority. She was damaged goods by '87. Came to Hollywood on the prestige train but five years later and she'd produced nothing but a handful of forgettable episodes on even more forgettable shows. I didn't see much of a future for her, and I figured, sure, let's do this Viking funeral style. Let's do a cancer arc on a show about a talking monkey! I was planning on dropping her as a client anyway.

Clark Francis, Writer: So the writing room's down to me and Sorrentino, and she comes in one day in January and shows me this leukemia screenplay that's clearly been gathering dust in her apartment for years. Trust me, I know. All writers have those scripts. And it's about this teenage couple where the girl gets leukemia and instead of being a supportive partner, the guy just gets introspective before realizing what a selfish prick he is a month after she dies. I guess the idea here is that we're all selfish pricks. It was bleak, and I had no idea how we could translate it to a kids' show about a talking monkey, but I was jazzed. We were going to get real with the kids just like back on *Update* with Chevy. I even tossed out the idea of casting Chevy as a new social studies teacher. He wanted to do it, I'm sure. He was probably just busy or something. Scheduling issues. You know how it goes with Chevy.

Gina Sorrentino, Writer: In my screenplay, I turned Maria and myself into a couple instead of best friends because I wanted to distance myself from reality. I wasn't ready to admit it was about Maria Aiello. I still don't like talking about her. Luckily, that synced perfectly with the show. Riley and Melissa were Li'l Einstein's best friends at Jane Goodall High, and they were also a couple. It felt like an omen.

Tommy America, Actor, from an interview in 1992 before his death: We got the scripts late. Like there's a cutoff point where if the principals don't get the scripts, the show doesn't get made. And Gina Sorrentino handed me the script like five minutes after that. She never personally delivered the scripts. Never. That was always our producer Vanessa Remington. But Gina told me she had to turn in the scripts late because she wanted to do something edgy, and if the network got hold of it too early, they'd demand all these changes. I was stoked. I was twenty-eight and playing a fifteen-year-old. I'd known Kirk Cameron from some commercial work in the late seventies, and he kept rubbing the success of *Growing Pains* in my face. He used to send me every teenybopper rag he made the cover of. I was like, hell yeah, I'll do your prestige arc about leukemia. I was Melissa's boyfriend. I had all the meaty parts. I'd finally stick it to Kirk Cameron once and for all.

Jenny Fingers, Actor: I was ecstatic when I read Gina Sorrentino's cancer scripts. We all knew the show was ending, and my team's goal was to transition me from a teen sitcom actress into a pop star. I'd recorded my album, *Hair Party in the Year 2000 with Jenny Fingers*, the previous fall, and the label was planning on dropping the single that summer. The timing was perfect. I finally had something to do on the show that wasn't just shaking my head at Mr. Buttons or Tommy America. Oh, and Gina didn't make me say my catchphrase even once. I really appreciated that. People still come up on the street and say it. They might as well carve that garbage onto my grave.

Brodie McKinnon, Head Moderator of the *Monkey High School* Fan Association Reddit: The leukemia arc is the most divisive topic in the *Monkey High School* fan community. We actually had to make a sticky on the boards for it, otherwise we'd need a whole sub-reddit to funnel all the Li'ls and RiLissas to. Oh, yeah. We call fans who prefer the first one-and-a-half seasons of the show Li'ls because those episodes focus on Li'l Einstein, and we call the fans of the leukemia arc RiLissas because those are all about Riley and Melissa. It's a divided community. There was even talk about MonHighCon being separated into two different conventions to placate the fan bases. It's a goddamn shame.

Dr. Claudia Fuhrmann, Professor of Television Studies at the University of Pittsburgh: A postmodern reading of *Monkey High School* reveals the final four episodes to be willingly complicit in their social critique of the universe of the simulacrum while also being entirely schooled in Marxist film theory. Curiously, these episodes make use of the modernist practice of calling attention to the materiality of the text by exposing its means of signification—a typically Brechtian critical technique.

Brodie McKinnon, Head Moderator of the *Monkey High School* Fan Association Reddit: So those last four episodes, right? In the first one, Melissa's acting weird and distant, and Riley thinks it's maybe because she's cheating on him with McGoober, the class clown. He goes to Li'l Einstein for advice, and this is really the last time Mr. Buttons has anything relevant to do on the show. That's why Li'ls hate the arc so much. It never resolves the thread about the CIA trying to find Li'l Einstein after he breaks out of Area 51 in the pilot. But yeah, Riley finally confronts her, and Melissa tells him she has leukemia. Then boom! Credits! And that's just the first episode of the arc. It's a total roller coaster!

Molly Reagan, Live Studio Audience Member: Yes, I was there when they recorded "Melissa's Secret." My entire family was. Our daughters were six and eight at the time, and we'd flown in from Carmel, Indiana, on vacation. Our youngest, Amy, was obsessed with TV, and we thought it'd be really encouraging for her to get a peek behind the scenes. The whole audience was shocked during the taping. Where was Li'l Einstein? Why didn't Melissa say her catchphrase? And that leukemia bit? Jeepers. Try explaining what leukemia is to a bunch of kids on their vacation. It was a show about a talking monkey, and not a very good one I might add. My two cents is the writers should have been blacklisted.

Brodie McKinnon, Head Moderator of the *Monkey High School* Fan Association Reddit: So then the leukemia arc jumps forward in time. Melissa's undergoing chemotherapy, and Riley's there every step of the way, but he's distant, you know? He thinks he should carry out this big, romantic gesture, but his heart isn't in it. He tells his dad he's totally positive Melissa loves him, but he isn't sure he loves her. But he can't tell her this because he's afraid it'll crush her. The third episode is the real tearjerker though. Riley and Melissa go to the movies, and Mel has to wear these paper boxes over her shoes and this weird surgical mask. The show transforms this super common high school experience into a total nightmare. But the worst part is when the movie ends. The darkness lifts and the show pans to all these teens chatting about football or prom, and Melissa turns to Riley and just matter-of-factly tells him that the doctors said she has to freeze her eggs otherwise she can never have kids even if she survives the disease.

Benjamin Whitmore III, Former Network President: I'm not going to sit here and tell you I did my due diligence during the final four episodes of *Monkey High School*. I didn't. I never reviewed the scripts. I didn't watch the dailies. I was up to my balls in some serious problems. Fox had just come online, and the battle with cable was really heating up. All the head honchos were basically hunkered down working on a relaunch of our major IPs for the fall of '87. We knew *Monkey High School* wouldn't be part of the rebranding. It fell through the cracks. Just for a month though. That was all Gina Sorrentino needed to ruin everything.

Vanessa Remington, Executive Producer: Everybody always wants to blame me for the last four episodes of *Monkey High School*. If network wasn't paying attention, I must have been, right? And yeah, I knew what Sorrentino was planning and that the network would be irate when word leaked. But you need to remember that the vast majority of the staff had defected over winter break and that everyone left behind knew they weren't going to be part of the fall '87 rebrand. They were cutting us loose, and really, everything that happened with Gina Sorrentino was the network's fault. They never should have given us those four final episodes. What did we need to wrap up? It was a kids' sitcom! But our original order was for twenty-two episodes, and they'd already cut us to eighteen by the third week of the second season. I think they really lacked programming for the spring and didn't want to scramble to fill our time slot. Our mid-season replacement was over budget and late.

Brodie McKinnon, Head Moderator of the *Monkey High School* Fan Association Reddit: "Doubt Thou the Stars are Fire" is the final episode, and it again jumps a year forward in time to Riley's graduation. Melissa doesn't appear for the first ten minutes, and for the first act the audience has to wonder whether or not she died offscreen between episodes. But then, right after graduation, Riley drives to a pawn shop and buys two wedding bands. We don't know what's happening, but then he goes to Melissa's house, and holy crap is it a shocking moment. Melissa is bald, thin, yellow, looks like she's about to die. This is supposed to be a kids' show!

Jenny Fingers, Actor: My only complaint about the leukemia arc was the last episode. Did makeup really have to make me look so . . . sick?

Brodie McKinnon, Head Moderator of the *Monkey High School* Fan Association Reddit: So Riley pops the question, and his voice is just empty. And Melissa says yes, but she doesn't look too psyched either. The two of them drive to Atlantic City which is another move the Li'ls hate because in the season one episode "Li'l Einstein and Death Valley," the show pretty directly states that *Monkey High School* takes place in Nevada, which makes sense when you start asking yourself just how far Li'l Einstein could have gotten after escaping Area 51 in the pilot. In "Doubt Thou the Stars are Fire," Atlantic City's only an hour away, so Sorrentino clearly disregards canon in the last episode which is a giant smoking gun for the Li'ls. Anyway, there's a flashback to Riley looking up into the stars and he just delivers this monologue where he says he doesn't want Melissa's death ruining the rest of his life, and he only knows one way to fix it. Then it cuts to their wedding in one of these shabby boardwalk chapels, and then the last scene of the entire series is on the beach. It's night, Riley and Melissa are alone, and both of them look absolutely miserable. There's this long silence, and for a moment, the viewer really thinks this is the note the show's going to go out on. But then Sorrentino really twists the dagger. Melissa turns to Riley and says . . .

EXCERPT FROM *MONKEY HIGH SCHOOL*,
"DOUBT THOU THE STARS ARE FIRE" SCRIPT:

```
    MELISSA
Let's not tell anyone, OK?

    RILEY
What?

    MELISSA
I don't want to tell anyone what we did here.
Let's keep it a secret.
```

RILEY
There's legal documents.

MELISSA
I want it kept a secret. This isn't what I imagined for my life. I don't mean the cancer. I mean you. I mean us. I mean us getting married.

RILEY
What's that supposed to mean? We talked about marriage even before.

MELISSA
I know that. But we're just kids. Do you realize how long the average life is? I might have lived till I was a hundred. You still might. I wasn't totally sure about us. I'm still not the person I might have grown into. Who knows if those people, our adult versions, would have been right together? I wanted so much more from my life than this. I had hopes and dreams totally independent from you.

RILEY
Melissa. I love you.

A long pause.

MELISSA.
I love you too, but we're not soulmates. I never really believed we'd get married. You should know that. I'm cold. Take me home.

Pan to stars. Credits.

Gina Sorrentino, Writer: I rewrote the final scene of "Doubt Thou the Stars are Fire" an hour before we filmed. In the screenplay version, the Melissa/Maria character is completely grateful that the Riley/Me character marries her even though they both know she's going to die. It ends with Riley/me feeling like he made a valiant gesture but also a mistake that's going to gnaw at him for the rest of his life. I wrote that when I was twenty-four, maybe twenty-five, and for the final episode, I just copied the final bits of dialogue. But then I really started looking at it and thinking about it and realized I still wasn't grieving for Maria Aiello, for everything she had lost. All I'd done was regurgitate my own introspective narcissism. I had to let Maria speak, allow her to claim that moment as her own, put all of her regrets on the table. And that's what I did. I know it sounds really stupid especially since it's a show about a talking monkey, but I put my heart on that fucking page. When I wrote the last line I was crying. I'd never cried for Maria before. It felt significant.

Felix Brown, Animal Handler: "Doubt Thou the Stars are Fire" is a disgrace.

Tommy America, Actor, from an interview in 1992 before his death: What did I think about the final scene? I thought that when Kirk Cameron saw my acting chops he was going to shit himself with envy.

Benjamin Whitmore III, Former Network President: I finally caught wind of Sorrentino's insurrection a month before sweeps. I'd been in Chicago scouting improv groups for something to rival NBC's stranglehold over Saturday nights, and when I got back, my secretary told me all these complaints had flooded in because of a *Monkey High School* episode. Now we never got mail for *Monkey High School*. Don't let the revisionists tell you it was a popular or important show. It wasn't. It was designed to be second or third tier. Something we could produce on the cheap to fill up a time slot until a better property came along. The first episode of the leukemia arc had just aired, and all these parents were complaining it wasn't an appropriate topic for a show aimed at kids in the 8 p.m. timeslot. So I watched the final four episodes, and trust me, it was not a difficult decision. I yanked the final three and scheduled game show reruns in their place. So what if *Monkey High School* ended on a cliffhanger? Garbage is interchangeable.

Clark Francis, Writer: I didn't really care one way or another if the final three episodes were pulled. That was really Sorrentino's pet project, and I got paid either way. I do remember my reaction when Vanessa Remington called and broke the news. I consumed a few too many 'shrooms and wandered out into the valley where I ran into Franken. He was pretty pissed at the networks in those days, and we got to talking and ended up buying these hogs and racing all the way to Vegas. I came to a week later naked on the shores of one of the Great Lakes. Can't remember which. So yeah, *Monkey High School*. Not a great time for ol' Clark Francis.

Gina Sorrentino, Writer: My reaction was that I'd failed. I felt like my entire life had been leading to that arc, and then nobody outside of a few dozen studio audience members ever saw it. I went into a tailspin after that and gave up writing, Hollywood, everything. I didn't even tell my agent. I just booked a flight back East and took a job as a guidance counselor at my old high school in Rochester. There's a Maria Aiello memorial plaque in one of the hallways. I've been here ever since.

Brodie McKinnon, Head Moderator of the *Monkey High School* Fan Association Reddit: If Whitmore hadn't pulled the final three episodes of *Monkey High School*, I don't think our fan community would even exist. I was nine years old when *Monkey High School* was canceled, and I remember crying when I realized we'd never learn what happened to Melissa or Riley. I even wrote my own ending where Li'l Einstein discovers a cure for cancer. We talked about it on the playground all the time. Why was this mostly forgettable show pulled off the air the very moment it introduced a serious plotline? I didn't know about the pockets of people all across the country wondering the exact same thing. But by my guess, there's at least two thousand of us *Monkey High* fans out there. Richie Bell started the first fan club via mailer, and he was the one who tracked down a master of the final three episodes at a studio auction. Bell was the one who transferred them to VHS and started selling copies at pop culture conventions.

Gina Sorrentino, Writer: Every few years I hear about the *Monkey High School* fan community and how they rescued the final three episodes and hand-distributed them. And then when the show was released on DVD last year, the producers included the last three episodes as bonus material and invited me to do audio commentaries. I didn't respond. What do I think about the fan community? Well, I know the last four episodes are divisive, and I know it's not really that large of a fan base. I guess I should be comforted that they're out there and some people like them, but I'm not. The most important work of my life is only enjoyed by a niche within a niche within a niche. When I'm honest with myself, when I really step back and evaluate everything that happened to me and what my goals were when I started, I can almost admit the truth. I never should have tried. That's what I honestly think. I never should have tried.

Do I Amuse You?

You probably don't know this, but there's a *Goodfellas* convention back East in Allentown, Pennsylvania, every August. I know because every day this summer I've driven thirty minutes to my office to watch *Goodfellas*. Then I watch it again. Then I research *Goodfellas* online. Then I drive home and cook a very elaborate meal from Marcella Hazan's *Essentials of Classic Italian Cooking*. When my wife gets off work and asks how my tenure portfolio's coming along, I tell her great, awesome, bellissimo. She doesn't know I haven't even started. She barely even knows what *Goodfellas* is.

• • •

Let me tell you about my favorite scene. Most fans opt for the Copa shot. Beginning at thirty-one minutes, thirty-one seconds into the film and set against the peppy "Then He Kissed Me" by The Crystals—a minor pop group on Philles Records, a Philadelphia label that only issued twelve full albums between 1962 and '72—the Copa shot follows protagonist/mobster Henry Hill and his new girlfriend Karen in an unbroken three-minute take as they enter the Copacabana through the backdoor. They weave through the kitchen and back channels of the club, and Henry seemingly knows everyone, slipping busboys cash and chatting up waiters, and Karen's reaction is the audience's reaction: bemused glee over discovering this hidden world where rules are broken and exceptions made, where average men are treated like kings simply because of their secret knowledge. It's an iconic sequence, and Terry Ratfoy, my colleague in what amounts for our film studies department, teaches it almost every semester, even in classes where, for one reason or another, he doesn't show *Goodfellas*.

Rebellious fans who push back against the Copa shot usually select either the introductions scene at the Bamboo Lounge or the sequence at the end of the film when Henry is finally arrested. The former is similar in spirit to the Copa shot. Starting at the sixteen minute and thirty-seven second mark, the introductions scene is yet another unbroken sequence where the camera takes on Henry's POV as he moves through the Bamboo Lounge. His voice-over introduces us to one gangster after another, and their onscreen counterparts make ironic statements like, "You staying out of trouble?" or "I took care of that thing for you." On the twenty-fifth anniversary Blu-ray commentary track, director Martin Scorsese says this scene is supposed to inspire nostalgia in the viewer, that the mobsters should appear like gods and that Henry, in retrospect, has now been cast out of paradise. The arrest scene, on the other hand, is a coked-out dose of sixties paranoia lifted straight out of Thomas Pynchon. Henry is driving all over town trying to sell guns while simultaneously prepping a drug run to Pittsburgh, making sauce and meatballs for his family, and being chased by a police copter. The scene strives for a dreamlike sensibility, and actor Ray Liotta plays the entire piece like a sweaty schizoid scanning the sky for a helicopter that only exists in his mind according to his mistaken friends. It feels like nothing else in the entire movie, and even the soundtrack acknowledges this. Gone are the pop hits of the fifties and sixties, replaced by the lesser known "Jump into the Fire" by Harry Nilsson off the 1971 RCA Victor classic, *Nilsson Schmilsson*. Even the album cover perfectly reflects the Watergate-inspired fear and loathing of Liotta's performance. It's just Nilsson in a ratty bathrobe in black-and-white, pipe in hand, refrigerator in background, hair sweaty and disheveled, a distant, morose look on his face like he's spent the last three days strung out while reading overdue conspiracy thrillers from the library. The arrest scene is pretty good is what I'm saying.

But my favorite scene begins fifty-seven minutes and six seconds in. Liotta, De Niro, and Pesci have just killed a made man and retreat to Pesci's mother's house. According to the clock we see in the dining room, it's a quarter after midnight, and yet, Pesci's mother is awake, played beautifully by Scorsese's real-life mother—this isn't the first time Scorsese's committed his mother to film; she was also the subject of his 1974 documentary *Italian-american* and plays yet another good-natured nonna in *Casino* made five years after *Goodfellas*—who demands they sit down for a full Italian meal. In a lesser film, this scene might be played purely for laughs. Here is the stereotypical Italian mother serving red sauce and meatballs to her grown son and pals in the middle of the night while meanwhile they have a body stashed in the trunk of Pesci's 1961 Chevy Impala. And while this scene *is* funny, there's something infinitely comforting about the way Catherine Scorsese implores Pesci to settle down with a nice woman while simultaneously pushing all three men to *mangia, mangia*. Maybe this sincerity lands because it's actually Martin Scorsese's mother, and when Catherine shows De Niro this absurd portrait she's produced of a rowboat with two dogs and an old man, your heart just breaks for her. She doesn't know that Pesci will soon be executed for the murder he just orchestrated. She doesn't know that this moment signals the end of her family. It's beautiful. It's personally meaningful. And I rewind it again and again and again in the darkness of my office. I rewind it again and again and again until the scene is reflected on my face, the stretched-out fuzzy mask of Catherine Scorsese staring lovingly at her fictional son, her real-life offspring watching from nearby, hidden as always behind the complicated machinery of the camera.

• • •

It's the end of August. I know this because suddenly the office is busy again. The English department shares a basement with Theology in ESCH, a rundown building on the south side of campus. It's usually empty in the summer minus the Chairs, admin, and me, but now I run into random faculty printing their syllabi while making bold proclamations about how this year will be different, that this year they'll finish their book, that this year they won't fall behind on grading within the first month of the semester. None of our offices have windows, so if you turn out the lights and shut the door, it's the perfect environment for watching *Goodfellas* on an otherwise unimpressive laptop. Another perk of watching from my office is that I have unfettered access to JSTOR, the biggest academic database in my field. Did you know that if you search for *Goodfellas* there are over five hundred articles and book chapters on JSTOR? My favorite is "Where Did the Goodfellas Learn to Cook? Gender, Labor, and the Italian American Experience" by Laura E. Ruberto in the summer 2003 issue of *Italian Americana*—pages 164-176. The essay problematizes the prison scene midway through the film where Liotta and the other captured mobsters make red sauce in prison, including an almost pornographic close-up of Paul Sorvino slicing garlic with a razor blade. I admire this essay, and I admire Ruberto, a tenured professor at Berkeley City College, and I try not to think about the connections between this essay and my own culinary experiments boosted by shortcuts I purchase at the Pasta and Market on 51th street.

The Chair knocks on the door and opens it before I can reply. "Knock, knock," she says through gritted teeth.

The Chair is Dr. Maya Wu. She does not want to be Chair and has made this very well known. But we're a small department—only six of us left—and after the previous Chair was struck down by stroke, Wu was tapped because she's the only one left with tenure. She immediately announced she would go on the job market in retaliation, and I assume she wants to be a Dean somewhere far from Indiana. "How's the tenure portfolio coming along?" she asks.

I flash two thumbs up.

"Great. Well, let me know if you want a letter of recommendation for the job market or anything. We probably won't be applying for the same jobs I hope."

I stare at Dr. Maya Wu. No one from the English department has earned tenure since I arrived six years ago. One year into the job, Wu staged a vague department rebellion against Business and Education—something about their request to decrease the core maybe; I don't know, I dozed off during the meeting—and a few months later the Chair of Education became the Dean of the College of Arts and Sciences and installed the Chair of Business as her Associate Dean. They harbored grudges and made it abundantly clear one of their goals was to turn our university into a technical school with no humanities core classes. That means the English department is redundant. That means I'm fucked no matter how much I publish, no matter how well I teach, that I should be applying to the three open jobs in my field nationwide, located in exciting places like Kentucky, Mississippi, and the Florida swamplands.

"The handbook says I'm supposed to check in and ask if you're ready to submit your tenure portfolio," Dr. Maya says. "Are you ready to submit your tenure portfolio next week?"

I say yes and wish I could see her face when the department discovers I've uploaded absolutely nothing. "Great seeing you," I say while shutting my door.

I return to my browser and stare longingly at the website for Allentown's *Goodfellas*Con, a two-day affair that's already underway. There's a panel on "the real story" behind the Lufthansa Heist—the MacGuffin that steers the plot in the film's final third—and Welker White, the actress who plays Henry's Pittsburgh drug courier, is scheduled to sign autographs. The only problem is the convention's in Allentown, and this is Indianapolis, and no matter how many times I've emailed the event staff at the Indiana Convention Center asking them to bring a *Goodfellas* convention to our humble city, I never get a reply. I decide to write them another email just in case—how can they justify hosting GenCon, an actual board game convention, over something *Goodfellas*-related—but I'm interrupted midway through by yet another knock at my door. I say, "Come in," but have half a mind to tell Dr. Maya how I really feel when Dr. Billy S. Witherspoon appears instead. The Chair of Theology has always looked to me like a retirement age Captain America. Chiseled jaw, majestically etched face, slightly graying hair, and—the coup de grâce—an actual leather jacket. I rise to shake his hand,

and Dr. Billy has the audacity to ask if I want to accompany him to Nicky Blaine's Cocktail Lounge, downtown Indianapolis's finest cigar bar.

"Yes," I say. "Absolutely. I can't wait."

• • •

I enjoy Nicky Blaine's Cocktail Lounge because it reminds me of the bars in *Goodfellas*. You have to descend this long flight of stairs just to enter, and everything is red and smoky, framed portraits of JFK and Lincoln hanging next to each other in back. Something about being underground makes me feel hidden and borderline dangerous, and the leather couches are all tacky and gauche, reminders of my Italian grandmother's home back in Scranton. Like always, Dr. Billy orders us both an Old Fashioned and a Gurkha Grand Reserve Churchill—a cognac infused cigar I've really grown to admire over the past few months. Dr. Billy teaches Lutheran theology to our confused undergraduates hailing from the cornfields of Indiana and, in a previous life, served as military chaplain in a semi-famous marine corp that did something vaguely heroic during the Vietnam War, but I can never remember exactly what. CBS made a TV movie about their exploits in 1993, and Dr. Billy showed it to me during the lone time he invited me and my wife for steaks and potatoes in his home out in the suburbs.

I really like Dr. Billy. I know I shouldn't, that he routinely pens articles against abortion and coed students living together and a million other freedoms I vehemently believe in, but Dr. Billy is so winning and charismatic that you can't help but treat him like the coolest brother you never had.

Dr. Billy lights our cigars, leans back in his leather sofa, and takes a long, relaxing puff. "Ah," he literally says, "now this is just a tiny bit of fantastic, isn't it?"

"Yes, Dr. Billy."

"'Yes' is right indeed!"

"Dr. Billy," I say, "did you know *Goodfellas* has an unofficial sequel?"

He leans forward, eyebrows arching. "Is that so?"

"*Goodfellas* is based on *Wiseguy*, a book by Nicholas Pileggi, who was married to Nora Ephron. Well, Nora wrote the script for *My Blue Heaven*, released one month prior to *Goodfellas*, which is based on Henry Hill's time in the Witness Protection Program. Hill's name is changed to Vinnie Antonelli in *My Blue Heaven* so people wouldn't get confused."

Dr. Billy considers this for a long time. "Is it any good?"

I shake my head vigorously. "No. It's supposed to be a comedy. Steve Martin is playing Vinnie, and he's doing this terrible and vaguely offensive impression of an Italian gangster. Rick Moranis stars in it too. Joan Cusack and Carol Kane are the love interests." I reach into my messenger bag. "I actually have the DVD with me if you want to watch it right now. I ordered it from the library. We can watch it on my laptop if you want."

Dr. Billy taps the ash from his cigar and gives me an extremely mischievous look. "No, I think I'm all right for right now, son. Maybe later though. I actually wanted to talk to you about something." He unlatches his briefcase and retrieves his earmarked Bible before setting it on the table between us. "I was hoping you gave some thought to my offer."

I pick up the Bible and thumb through it. These biweekly bull sessions at Nicky Blaine's Cocktail Lounge started six months ago after my parents died. Before that, Dr. Billy was cordial to me in the office but never went out of his way to invite me out. After news spread throughout the basement he appeared in my office one snowy afternoon with marked-up copies of my meager publications, lackluster essays attempting to reorient the work of late twentieth century American realists—Carver, Dubus, Mason, Pancake—as postmodern anti-fables through a Deluze and Guattari anticapitalist lens. My work is derivative and forced—I knew this even in graduate school but was determined to make good and become a scholar—and Dr. Billy suffered through a few questions about my essays during those initial cigars before pivoting into my family background and my parents' deaths. He assured me again and again that he'd been a military chaplain and knew how to council young men. The truth was I wanted to go into therapy but was ashamed to admit this to my wife. She didn't believe in it, and, instead, steered me to one of her coworkers at IU Health who put me on 40 milligrams of Propranolol, a remedy for "acute anxiety" that did absolutely nothing. So, that first afternoon smoking cigars with Dr. Billy, I told him everything—about growing up Italian in rundown Scranton, how I escaped my origins to earn a PhD in twentieth century literature despite the fact that neither of my parents even went to college, how they died in a car crash on the way to visit us in Indiana because I'd been too cheap, too stupid, too much of a little shit to pay for their flights. I talked and I talked and I talked and, at the end, Dr. Billy asked me if I'd pray with him. I never did—who knew where it might end and if Dr. Billy would force me at gunpoint to become a deacon—but I was tired of disappointing him, my only friend in the entire Midwest.

"Your offer to pray together?" I ask to make sure we're on the same page.

He winks. "You got it, big fella."

I take a long pull from my Old Fashioned.

"It won't hurt anybody," he says. "Just one little prayer. I bet it'll probably make you feel better too. More so than watching *Goodfellas*, am I right? Har har!"

I say nothing, and Dr. Billy takes this as consent. He puts my hands into his own, bows his head, and closes his eyes. It feels weird to have an adult man touch me, and I want to tell him this, but I don't know how, and I can't keep my eyes closed, so I stare at the picture of JFK. The assassinated president is petting a very large dog.

"Oh, lord," Dr. Billy says, "thank you for this wonderful bounty you've set up for us today. These fine cigars and two beautiful Old Fashioneds. And thank you for friendship and for putting me on the path to meeting this fine young man right here in good ol' Nicky Blaine's. We'd like to pray for the souls of his parents, two charming Italians from Scranton, Pennsylvania."

I stop listening when he pronounces it eye-talians. I feel very far away and finally decide to close my eyes and try this thing I do when I can't fall asleep. I play a little movie in my head and attempt to recreate it shot for shot. I see Ray Liotta's face that could be my father's or cousin's or uncle's, and I hear him say, "As far back as I can remember, I always wanted to be a gangster," and I feel something approximating relief.

• • •

I'm home by three o'clock, thank god, because this is just barely enough time to make the sauce and the gnocchi and the meatballs. I open the Marcella Hazan cookbook on the dining room table and stream the *Goodfellas* soundtrack from my phone to the Bluetooth. Making this food, the Italian food I never made growing up, is the closest I come to feeling like I still have family. I start with the sauce. Cut the onions, sauté them in olive oil, then, when they're almost translucent, I toss in the garlic and the fresh parsley. I've experimented with all kinds of tomatoes—organic Romas from the co-op, ruby red 'matoes from the farmers' market, cans of San Marzanos imported straight from Italy—and the latter works best. I buy them in bulk from the Pasta and Market and dump them in right before the garlic browns, breaking them up with my wooden spoon. I lower the heat, cheat with some tomato paste and maybe a slug of red wine depending on what we have on hand, then it's onto the gnocchi, the boiling of potatoes, the mashing, the whisking off eggs and flour. A little fork to make indentations so the sauce will actually adhere to the gnocchi—nothing is more offensive to me then gnocchi without indentations. I fill up two baking trays, slide them into the refrigerator, and next come the meatballs and two critical junctures: 1) lay a piece of white bread into the frying pan on low heat with half-a-cup of milk. Cook until it's absorbed the milk and mash in your mixing bowl with the ground meat and egg and pepper and salt. And 2) after rolling your meatballs, coat them in bread crumbs. This locks in the moisture.

I cook and cook and cook and I'm sweating like a triathlete, but for once I'm actually happy. The thing about Italian food is that it's not about food. The food is a conduit. The food is a time machine. The food brings everyone back albeit momentarily. The food is the gesture of a foolish heart. The food proves that you're willing to go through the extra trouble of making everything from scratch when you could just buy prepackaged and jars—sort of what Karen means in *Goodfellas* when she says, "I was even proud that I had the kind of husband who was willing to go out and risk his neck just to get us the little extras." I make the sauce and gnocchi and meatballs and feel briefly returned to that warm little kitchen on Sunday afternoons, when I'd come in from baseball around the corner and find my parents happily stirring a pot of sauce, a room that still feels like the center of love in this strange metallic world. I cook and feel righted.

Angelina arrives at seven, like always. She removes her orthopedic sneakers in the doorway, smells the food, and says, "Red sauce again?" And I say nothing because of course it's red sauce again. Red sauce only smells like red sauce, and we're both Italian, so she should know. Angelina's a nurse at IU Health, and we've been married for three years. I met her in Pittsburgh when she was a senior and I was a graduate student teaching Seminar in Composition to drowsy freshmen. We had an easy back and forth, light, jokey conversations. There was never a good reason for us to break up, so when I was offered the Indy job and Angelina said she'd only move with a man who proposed, it all made a certain kind of sense. Now, I glance out at her from the kitchen and can see there were probably better, alternative paths for us. I haven't told her about my empty dossier, but she knows that if I'm denied tenure, I will lose my job and we will have to move. She knows, and I know, and we do not speak of this. I wonder if she also is imagining a future where we are finally brave enough to admit all our buried truths.

Angelina enters the kitchen in her nurse's uniform and pushes against me, and I brush the hair from her forehead and kiss the top of her head. I remember Paulie in *Goodfellas*, when he tells Henry he has to go back to his wife, that he "will straighten this thing out. I know just what to say to her. I'm going to tell her you're going to go back to her and everything's going to be just how it was when you were first married. There's going to be romances, and it's going to be beautiful." Henry's face is completely unbelieving, and I get it, understand it, even though I don't want to, even though I know how awful I am, the kind of man who would ask his parents to drive ten hours to save a few hundred bucks.

"I made gnocchi," I say.

"I can see that," she says.

• • •

The next morning, I drive to work and listen to *Goodfellas Minute* on the way. It's a podcast where each episode takes an extended look at a single minute in *Goodfellas*. The episodes are in chronological order and there are 146 episodes in all, one for each minute of the film. Every episode is around forty minutes long, and I've made my way through the first ninety-six, landing me in the Christmas party following the Lufthansa Heist, the moment when everything starts to fall apart for our antiheroes. I'm so enthralled by the episode that, at first, I don't even realize I've missed my exit for the university. By the time I do, I'm in between exits and decide to drive just a little bit more so I can extend my time with this particular episode. What does it matter anyway? No one's keeping track of my hours at work, and it's not like I'm actually doing anything. I'm just watching *Goodfellas* and waiting for Dr. Billy to invite me out for cigars. So, I listen and sail past the next exit, then the next and the next. When the episode ends, I think, OK, big fella, this is it. Fun romp. But now it's time to turn around and head to work. But cellphones are a kind of magic and without me even having to do anything, it sucks the next episode out of the sky, and then it's playing on my stereo. Episode ninety-seven about minute ninety-seven, a continuation of that wonderful Christmas scene. OK, I think. "OK," I say to no one. Another episode and a nice, head-clearing drive out in the country.

But then a funny thing happens when episode ninety-seven ends. I realize I'm on I-70, the same road where my parents died. My father was always an aggressive driver and would routinely terrify me and my mother on the curving two-lane highway that led out of Scranton into the sprawling capitalism of Dickson City. I should have known that removing him from the small and familiar and setting him loose on a cross-country superhighway would end in disaster, but, like always, I was selfish. They died outside South Vienna, Ohio, a tiny town between Dayton and Columbus. I'd never been there before, had refused the pictures, but understood that my dad had been driving in the blind spot of a mack truck for miles, and the driver forgot they were there, merged into the passing lane, and sent my parents' ancient Oldsmobile careening into the concrete divider where they were killed on impact. I've been driving for almost ninety minutes and realize South Vienna is only forty-five minutes away, just enough for episode ninety-eight of *Goodfellas Minute*. What the hell, I think. Let's see where my parents died!

So, here comes South Vienna, and it's just an absolute nothing, nada, zilch. Flat and green like the rest of this particular stretch of the Midwest, and then a McDonald's rolls into view, and I'm so angry my parents were killed near a McDonald's that I floor the gas, and now I'm driving 80, 90, 100 miles per hour, and I remember Joe Pesci in the scene where he drunkenly shoots Spider's foot and yells, "*The Oklahoma Kid*! That's me! I'm the Oklahoma Kid, you fucking varmint! Dance! Dance, you motherfucker!" and then I become very loud and shout, "*The Oklahoma Kid*! That's me! I'm the Oklahoma Kid, you fucking varmint! Dance! Dance, you motherfucker!" and then I repeat it and repeat it and I keep driving and I don't stop and I just keep going until I see the flat earth ascend into mountains.

• • •

The Allentown Hilton is smaller than I imagined. All those weeks and months picturing *Goodfellas*Con, and it's just a few blocked-off rooms for panels and a large, open space where dealers sell memorabilia. I'm grateful I can still buy tickets at the door, and I stupidly tell the guy in the Scorsese T-shirt who hands me a lanyard that I drove all the way from Indiana just to be here. "It just happened," I say through a smile. "I was on my way to work, and then ten hours later here I am!" He looks me up and down and says, "Big whoop. I flew from Alaska." So I rebound and say, "You're really funny. You know that? The way you tell the story. The way you talk," and it's not a perfect line reading from the film, but he gets it, smiles, and says, "Have a ball, amigo!"

I wander the convention floor and look at *Goodfellas* action figures and signed scripts and T-shirts and even a briefcase like Dr. Billy's except this one has Ray Liotta's cackling face painted on the side. Everyone here looks like they could be my cousin. We're all Italian and this feels to me like the worst reunion in the world. I do a lap, and I'm about to hightail it back to my Nissan when I recognize something on a vendor's table. It's a replica of Catherine Scorsese's painting in the midnight pasta scene—a rowboat carrying two dogs and a fisherman. I run my hands up and down the cheap frame and ask the vendor how much and he tells me five hundred and I know that's insane but I reach for my wallet and hand him my credit card. So now I'm carrying this enormous painting like a big dumb idiot and that's when I see the sign for Welker White, the actress who played Lois. I'd almost forgotten! I follow the signs out of the convention hall and into a tiny blocked-off room with Welker White chatting up her handler behind a table. There's no line to speak of, and I can barely believe my luck.

In the film, Welker White's Lois is a bit part. But she appears in the famous arrest scene so she's well remembered by fans. Now, she's in her fifties wearing a smart pantsuit, her platinum hair cropped short, big earrings bookending her face. In front of her is a tower of glossies, and I can't believe it but she reminds me of my mother, a woman like Catherine Scorsese who would implore me to *mangia, mangia* even if it was midnight and I'd just eaten a six-course meal. I'm trembling beneath the weight of this replica of Catherine's painting, and I approach Welker White, and she says hello, and I say hello, and then I stupidly tell her that *Goodfellas* is my favorite movie ever.

"Oh, really?" Welker White says. "Why?"

I shift under the weight of the painting. I can barely believe it, but no one has ever asked me this before. At first, I try to intellectualize it and problematize it like Dr. Laura E. Ruberto in "Where Did the Goodfellas

Learn to Cook?" or even how I try with Carver or Dubus or Mason or Pancake. I want to say something witty and intelligent about how *Goodfellas* mythologizes the desire of the common man to stand outside the regular rules and regulations of society, making it an unwitting Marxist critique of capitalism. But then I decide to be honest with myself. What do I like about it? I stare at Welker White for a very long time, her face transitioning from good-natured cheer to just a whiff of tension, fear that maybe there's something wrong with me. I reach out to shake her hand, but she just looks at me and repeats her question. Again, I don't reply, so her middle-aged handler says, "Sir. Sir. Did you hear Ms. White? Are you OK?"

I look at him, then back at Welker White. I smile as wide as I can. I tell them, "I like *Goodfellas* because it fills the shape of my depression," and it's the first honest thing I've said in a very long time.

Take It Out of Me

The clinic looks nothing like what I expected. High ceilings. Gaudy Christmas lights. New age saxophone pumped in from all directions. I follow the nurse through the open floor plan and avoid looking at the patients on the examination tables. She leads me to the far end of the room and smiles. It's just Thursday for her.

"Can I . . . keep my clothes on?" I ask.

Another grin. "First time, huh?"

I start to blush but will it back. I remember my accomplishments, my modest yet impressive home in Eden Prairie, the degrees framed in my office, the books on my shelves with my name on their spines. This nurse is maybe six months out of college, and I remind myself I have nothing to be afraid of. "You might say that," I manage.

"No need to disrobe today," she explains. "That comes later. Dr. Park will be with you shortly, Ms. Rinaldi."

I sit on the examination table and swipe email on my phone, each message from students shocked they've received Ds or Cs after missing full weeks of my courses. I'm so absorbed that I almost miss Dr. Park extend her hand. She's a twenty-something, closer to my graduate students than me, her oval glasses smudged.

"Pleasure to meet you, Ms. Rinaldi," she says in a high, pleasant tone.

"Dr. Rinaldi," I correct her.

"Doctor. That's right. Of course." She picks up my chart and taps her chin. "So, this is your first visit with us, correct?"

"Correct."

"Before we begin, do you have any questions?"

I straighten the lapels of my jacket. "Does it actually work?"

She tilts her head. Kenny G launches into an extended solo on the speakers above us. "Does what work?"

"This. All of this."

She smiles in a way she must think is reassuring. "Absolutely. We're the finest class reimaging facility in Minnesota, and this is our ninth year serving the community. We've successfully erased thousands of working-class memories and traits out of our patients and have implanted close to the same number. Middle-class memories, upper-class, we tailor a program that's right for you."

I've read all this online, scanned the many testimonials, but something about the flesh-and-blood Dr. Park saying it makes it feel so much more real. "So, just to be clear, you go in, locate some kind of working-class memory or trait I tell you about, and funnel it out?"

"In a certain kind of sense, yes."

"And then, if I choose, you can replace those memories or traits with aspects that more closely align with middle or upper-class experiences?"

"Absolutely." Dr. Park waggles her eyebrows. "It's a wonderful process." She opens the shelving unit behind her and retrieves a thin cylinder resembling a powder blue sex toy. "You tell us everything you want removed, and everything you'd like inserted, and then we numb your whole head and slide one to five of these inside of you depending on how much work you'd like done in a single session. Then you go home and over a weekend your memories and traits manifest themselves in any number of unpleasant but temporary ways. Hemorrhoids. Broken teeth. Jock itch. Warts. You come back forty-eight hours later, we put you under, remove all your manifested issues, and suddenly, you don't remember Uncle Mort's racist Thanksgiving tirade or how you had to wear Salvation Army hand-me-downs to college. It's barely more invasive than getting your teeth cleaned."

I twist my wedding band around my finger. "Have you ever done it?"

Dr. Park pats my knee. "Dr. Rinaldi, I don't even remember what state I was born in anymore. It's absolutely awesome!" She removes a pen from behind her ear and brings it to the clipboard. "Let's chat out your specific needs a bit. Do you want removal, insertion, or both?"

"Both."

She checks a box. "What specific things do you want removed?"

I pull up my notes on my cellphone. "I don't want to remember all my class shame from college, all those parties where I wore the wrong clothes, wrong shoes, where I didn't know how to handle myself around cheese and crackers. I don't want to remember my mother crying about how we were headed to the poor house every few months growing up. Erase all those days at my father's deli answering calls, serving men in suits from the courthouse, the smell of lunchmeat and mayonnaise and toasted bread in my hair. Take away the nostalgia I have for twangy country music, Willie Nelson, light beer. Take away the confused looks from my family at holidays when I told them I was studying Italian in college. Take away their refusal to come to my wedding because it was a three-hour drive from home and 'too far.' Take away every time a colleague referenced growing up on NPR and summers in Cape Cod and how I smiled and politely nodded but wanted to choke them. Take away the years of being poor, the years of feeling poor, the stress of past due bills, the years without insurance, the realization that everyone I thought was upper class growing up because they owned a pool or two cars was actually just lower middle class, take away how I feel less than everybody else." I continue for fourteen minutes. "Take away the knowledge that my brother died from a drug overdose."

Dr. Park nods. "OK. That's a lot, but it's doable. And insertions?"

"I don't know anything about wine or classical music. Fix that. I'd like to know more about professional women's fashion, how investing works, how retirement works. Basically, I'm just so sick and tired of feeling like an impostor every single second of every single day."

Dr. Park nods sympathetically. "You won't feel that anymore, Dr. Rinaldi. I promise." She checks more boxes. "What you're proposing is a bit more intensive than what I usually recommend for first-timers. Would you rather we do this over a few visits?"

I shake my head. "No. I'm not teaching during J-Term. I want this done before I start again in February." This is an excuse, a vague justification, but I know most people never question the mysterious schedule of academics.

She frowns. "OK. We can manage that, but are you absolutely sure? You're positive you want to remove everything you've listed?"

"Take it out of me."

• • •

Dinner is a skillet-roasted chicken alongside potatoes and carrots cooked in animal fat. My husband calls this his "working man's dinner," and I let him live out this ridiculous fantasy. We never used a skillet growing up or indulged on an entire bird outside of Thanksgiving and once spent an entire summer eating the overgrown zucchini my father grew in our backyard. But Henry is a good cook, and that counts for something, and I watch from the dining room as he brings me a plate and feel thankful for his stabilizing presence, the way he refills the white wine I pretend to like, the way he punches in Berlioz's *Symphonie fantastique* on his phone and how it plays everywhere in our house on this expensive Bluetooth system Henry is obsessed with. I touch his hand when he sits down. He's always been fascinated by machines. I don't understand any of it—why bury your face in a computer when there are books?—but I love him. I've always known this.

He waits until we're midway through our meal before confronting me. It's another benefit of his upbringing. Where I grew up, fights began in the kitchen before the sauce was even bubbling. "I know you're going to do this no matter what I think," Henry says, "but I wish you'd wait until the conference was over."

Next week is the Digital Humanities Winter Institute. Henry and a host of other professors interested in the digital from all over North America will embark upon a small Canadian island off the coast of Seattle to learn new programs and debate digital Marxist theory at the University of Victoria. Henry is going to study digital computing and desktop fabrication, and although he's explained this to me many times, I still have no idea what it means. I scheduled my two appointments with Dr. Park while he's in Canada. "Henry, I want to deal with this alone."

"I'm your husband."

"And I love you."

"Then let me help you."

"You'll help me by going to Victoria."

He pouts into his food. He's never known how to deal with my insecurities. He grew up in London where his father is a reputable hedge fund manager. My upbringing is completely alien to him, and after a few visits back home to meet my family, he prefers it that way. We've worked hard to earn tenure here in Minnesota, both at the same prestigious college, he in mathematics, myself in Italian language and literature. We've cast off the shackles of my origins, or I'm at least trying to.

He clears our plates, the Berlioz nearly complete. Then he returns and pulls me up from my chair and slides his arms around my waist. I know he wants sex, and I want it too, how all our problems briefly melt away, but then Henry looks into my eyes and whispers, "What if we have a child? Don't you want them to know how you grew up?"

We've gone back and forth on the baby issue more times than I can count. Sometimes I want one, sometimes he wants one, but usually we both agree it's not for us. We watch the news, read about climate change, and cannot imagine leaving behind spawn to deal with the calamities of previous generations. I look at my husband and understand some things between us will always remain unknowable. I want to explain to him very clearly that I'm doing this precisely because of the off chance we might have a child. I don't want that hypothetical baby to ever understand a single moment of what I endured to get here, how alienated I felt in high school—my dreams and aspirations even then so different from my peers—in college—my background and material wealth so minuscule compared to the others—and even now—when I have literally no one to talk to who shares the same cultural touchstones of my youth. I don't want that child to know any of this, and I need to cleanse myself completely to shield them from everything I know I am at my core. But I can't say this to sweet Henry who believes in me, loves me, adores me, even when I don't understand why. He'd take it as a personal failure.

I press my head into the crook of his shoulder and whisper into his neck, "You'll remember for both of us," and I know he won't and for this I am truly, utterly grateful.

• • •

A week later, after depositing Henry at the airport, I drive to the clinic, disrobe, and return to Dr. Park's examination table. Soon, they're all around me, angels in powder blue, injecting syringe after syringe into the flesh of my neck. I become extremely calm and can almost feel myself floating above my body. I watch as Dr. Park taps the cylinder that will go inside me to the beat of Kenny G. She winks at a nurse who stretches my mouth open as far as it will go. Then they insert the metal clamp, and I am so drugged and so happy that I literally think, golly golly, which is a catchphrase my best friend in high school—Norma Fernandez—came up with to express ironic astonishment at our teachers, peers, family. Norma switched from part-time to full at Target after we graduated, and although we stayed in touch for a few years after, we surrendered by our midtwenties. I know from social media that she now has three sons, and I wonder if she's ever left the state. Golly golly, I think, as Dr. Park slides the first cylinder down my throat and into my stomach, then the second, third, fourth, fifth. Golly golly. Golly golly. Golly golly!

• • •

The Great British Bake Off is my favorite TV show. Henry has rigged our television with dozens of machines I don't want to understand, our coffee table a fortress of remote controls. But I know exactly what to do to stream *The Great British Bake Off*, and that's what I'm doing the morning after my procedure. *The Great British Bake Off* is a cooking competition where ordinary British citizens compete to win the favor and admiration of two pastry chefs—one, a legendary home cook who resembles an idealized version of a white grandmother, the other, Britain's version of a hip middle-aged man who is completely insufferable. I've never liked American reality TV because there's so much hyperbole, so much yelling and arguing that it reminds me of my childhood, that cramped home, the screaming matches, the constant fighting over money. But *The Great British Bake Off* is the gentlest TV show I've ever seen. Everyone, even the losers, are praised, and the delicious treats they bake so quickly, so expertly in their giant circus tent look so beautiful that you can't help but feel pleasure when the grandmother carves into them with her knife. Even the contestants are whimsical and carefree. Finalist Gina reminds me of my upper-class students, not a care in the world, in love with life, total confidence that they will be successful at whatever impractical enterprise they set their minds to. I watch her and feel envy, pride, rage. I want to slip through the television and tell her how I grew up. I want to ask her how it's fair that I had to crawl my way to publication and the professoriate in the most undignified fashion possible while she was born whole on television, pristine and perfect and ready for a new blessing with each new second. I watch fourteen episodes in a row, and then Henry calls from Victoria.

"How are you feeling?" he asks.

I have avoided looking at myself in the mirror, but this is what I know. My feet are covered with warts. Crusty. If I dig in with my fingers or a Q-tip, I can extract hardened puss, dead skin, I don't know? But I can't get beyond the ringed craters left behind. I can barely sit down because my anus is filled with hemorrhoids—the blood in the toilet confirms this—and I briefly considered having a hemorrhoid pillow delivered to our home via drone. My teeth are in so much pain I fantasize about ripping them out of my skull with pliers. Instead, I've read online that if you swish mouthwash in your mouth for three minutes, the alcohol will numb your teeth. So I do that every hour. The joint in my right knee is throbbing. My face is covered with acne. There's an itchy rash running up and down my back and along my inner thighs. Gas stabs my lower abdomen, and acid reflux returns every bite I eat to the base of my throat. This, Dr. Park assured me, is normal. This is the process of my origins rising out of me.

"I've never felt better," I tell Henry over the phone. "I really feel quite beautiful."

• • •

The second procedure is easier than the first. The hardest part is transporting my bloated, disgusting body from our home in Eden Prairie back to the clinic in St. Paul. I'm worried about the car's upholstery, if I will have time to clean it before Henry returns from Canada, face red with the excitement of having learned how to do something new and mysterious with machines. It's extremely difficult to drive, and I almost call a Lyft, but I can't bear the thought of someone else seeing me in my condition, so I drive very slowly on the side streets, along Minnehaha Parkway and the ice-covered lakes and frosted parks. At the clinic, Dr. Park attaches a mask over my mouth and nose and says, "I went through this too you know. I wish I could experience it for the first time all over again. You're lucky," she says. "You're so very lucky."

I wake up an hour later on the examination table, the same Kenny G overhead. In the shelving unit I see eight separate jars filled with green liquid, formaldehyde I assume. Little pieces of me swim inside—pimples, warts, broken teeth, fleshy mushrooms that must be working-class tumors. There it is, I think. That's what lived inside of you for so long. But then I remember my dead brother, the deli, Norma Fernandez, and I begin to panic.

Dr. Park hurries over, Starbucks in hand. She sees my dread and waves it away. "It's OK if you still remember," she announces. "It's not instantaneous. Give it two hours max, and you'll be fine. You'll be everything you ever wanted."

I sit up and feel sore, but nothing more serious than a particularly long day at the gym—something I've avoided the last few years. Dr. Park holds a mirror to show me that all evidence of my procedure is gone minus the bags under my eyes, nothing a long night's sleep won't cure. She's about to extend the curtain so I can dress and leave, but then I feel a tightening in my chest, something new and unexpected, the way Henry describes his occasional panic attacks. I dig my nails into my knees and watch Dr. Park move toward my jars.

"What are you going to do with them?" I ask.

She looks confused and points at the jars. "These?"

I nod.

"We dispose of them in an eco-friendly way if that's what you're worried about. We have an incinerator in the basement."

The question is out of my mouth before I can consider the ramifications or if this is even what I really want. "Can I have them?"

Again, Dr. Park is mystified. "The jars? They're just medical waste."

"I know, but can I have them?"

"I'm not sure—"

"I'm taking them. I'll pay you. Just let me have them."

Dr. Park blinks. She blinks again. "OK. You can have them. I'll have someone bring them out to your car. But don't blame us if something goes wrong, Dr. Rinaldi."

• • •

I regret my decision before I'm even on 94. I look into the rearview mirror, and there they are, jars of my filth, my imperfections, buckled in like eight hideous children. I speed and speed and try not to think. Henry is returning from Victoria tomorrow. What am I going to do with these jars? Why would I even want these jars of waste?

In Eden Prairie, I park in our garage, but I don't remove the jars from the vehicle. Instead, I go inside. I pace the living room. I look upon our shelves and shelves of books. I remove my first book and flip to the photo of me in the back. There I am, I say. I wrote a book. This is evidence. This is my face. Younger, but me. I open my second book and confirm my face there as well. Then I pace, pace more. I go into the basement where Henry has assembled a small wooden wine rack. He's a fan of the Valenti Norma Etna Rosso, a charming red comprised of grapes grown in black volcanic soil, notes of balsamic and baking spice and blue flower. But I opt for the Clarendon Hills Liandra Syrah—black crimson, peat, bitter chocolate—the go-to glass of perfection I've adored all my life since my mother gifted me a bottle at college graduation. It tastes like home, memory, the confidence of everything I was groomed for, and I'm mildly ashamed to drink it from the bottle, but I need to think, need to understand everything I've done. I return upstairs and manage to start Henry's Bluetooth speaker contraption. I cast Tobias Humes's *Poeticall Musicke*, a beautiful 1607 cello piece my brother introduced me to last year over dinner and drinks with his young family in the vineyard. I am sweaty. I am confused. I listen to the cello and appreciate its deep notes, the artistry of Humes's longing. I understand it and always have. I return to the garage and know exactly what I will do even though it's ten degrees below freezing, even though I am a professor of Italian language and literature and physical labor has always been beneath me. I open the back door, and I put my outer winter layers on one piece at a time—the scarf, the parka, the hat, my gloves. Then I pick up Henry's shovel and step into the darkness. Everything is quiet, still, just the swirling of flurries, the low swept vistas of icy apocalypse. I penetrate the ground with the shovel and push it deeper with my boot. Then I dig and I dig and I dig. I dig deeper than I ever thought possible. I dig a new world there in our once familiar yard, and when it's ready, when everything is finally ready for me, I return to the car and carry my jars of imperfections one after another to their final resting place. Goodbye! I shout. Goodbye! I have an instinct to say golly golly, but I don't know why, so I don't say it, and instead I chuck the final jar in and bury them one shovelful of snow and dirt at a time until no one anywhere has to know about what I was and what I am and everything I still might become. I stand there shivering and drinking and allow myself to imagine Henry's hypothetical child and how I will hold that baby in my hands and say I will protect you from all of this and you will never know about any of this over my dead fucking body you will never know about the dirt and the blood and the shit I emerged from you will never know you will never know you will never fucking know any of that dead gone world you sweet sweet child of mine.

Mamma-draga

Frank bought the skateboard seven weeks after his divorce. It gave him something positive to focus on even before it arrived, when it was only a tracking number, a link to refresh late at night when Frank blinked himself awake and remembered he was no longer in his split-level, but instead his childhood bedroom in Squirrel Hill. He reached for his cellphone on those sleepless nights and flooded the tiny room with artificial light. There it appeared, the Crimson Cross 8″ x 31.5″ preassembled skateboard moving in an unbroken line across America headed straight for Frank Catalano, fresh divorcé.

He sliced through the packing tape when it finally arrived, raising the board high above his head like something holy. As a teen at the turn of the millennium, Frank had goofed around with skateboards like the rest of his athletic friends, would clip a Discman to his jeans and sail across those inky black parking lots. Even then he couldn't compare to the best skaters of Central Catholic, kids who effortlessly grinded rails and impressed the girls who smelled permanently of patchouli. Frank was captain of the hockey team and occasionally landed a successful kickflip while his best friend Rocco hooted from the trunk of his car.

So it wasn't nostalgia that summoned Frank back to skateboarding, but something more difficult to convey. He'd deleted most of his social media accounts after the divorce. He knew what he'd find there and couldn't bear scrolling past Amy mugging in her new house or posing with her brand-new hybrid car. But Frank held onto Instagram because he never uploaded pictures and hadn't added a single friend. Instead, he went by the anonymous BlackAndGold1984_Guy and confined himself to the discover tab and its surprising number of hockey reels. Each time he liked a video of some rando landing a trick shot, the algorithm would remember and beam related topics his way. This eventually led him to skateboarding and the many reels of daredevils attempting goofy-foot nollies over car-sized gaps. He had no illusions about leaping gaps himself. Pickup games at the Ice Complex kept him in shape, but he was still a thirty-six-year-old man who drank a case of Yuengling every week. But if he could just skateboard again and balance the weight of his body on that wooden board for even a handful minutes, then he could definitively prove to himself that he was headed in the right direction and not a fool for nurturing hope for the future.

Frank tucked the new skateboard under his arm and climbed into his sedan, a Saturn with a quarter-million miles on the odometer. The art under the board depicted a bloody cross guarded by ghosts. Nothing macabre. Just some ragtag Caspers like kids on Halloween wearing bedsheets with their eyes cut out. He'd chosen this board on impulse, grateful for that familiar rush of endorphins, the chemical happiness produced whenever he "did a capitalism" like his Gen Z coworkers teased. Frank zipper merged onto the highway and drove to the suburbs, steering into a boarded-up strip mall.

Thanks to a dozen how-to videos on YouTube, Frank knew exactly how to position himself on the board above the smooth pavement, how to lead with his right foot and push off with his left, how to swivel his sneakers in the proper direction. All this was muscle memory, and Frank felt deeply reassured by how easily it returned, how quickly he picked up speed and carved circles just by crouching and leaning slightly to the left. Skating made him feel like a tiny bird had hatched inside his body, a delicate secret that flushed his cheeks. Frank couldn't kickflip or ollie or grind, but he could at least propel himself forward. That, more than anything else, was something worth living for.

• • •

Frank sprained his ankle two weeks later, but what a glorious period it was. What he loved most about his new life as a skateboarder was how dramatically it transformed his worldview. Before skateboarding, Frank drove to work on autopilot, zoning out to hockey podcasts or talk radio. Mondays through Thursdays, Frank was as an office temp for a shipping company in the suburbs. But since that was only part-time, he also picked up hours at Trader Joe's, tearing open cartons of orange chicken or palak paneer, working just long enough for the benefits. He rarely noticed his surroundings because he'd lived in Pittsburgh all his life and knew its bridges and curves as intimately as the topography of Amy's body. But as a skateboarder, he found himself noting every empty lot he passed. This wasn't blight; it was opportunity! Skateboarding filtered his reality, and patches of Pittsburgh he'd never truly noticed before—a sloping set of rails off Park Avenue, the curved ledges by the post office—pulsed alive with wonder and possibility. During those magical two weeks, Frank rode every day. He even bought a pair of Nike Blazers popular on r/Skateboarding and admired his transformation in his bedroom mirror, how powerful he now appeared.

Frank knew from Reddit that everyone fell and that it was better to get it over with. But after his initial success, he tricked himself into believing that he was perhaps the exception, a former athlete with unusual control over his body. It wouldn't have been so bad if he fell doing something cool. But instead, he was skating very slowly through a Dollar Tree parking lot when he attempted to kick turn around a patch of gravel. The board shot out from under his Blazers, and Frank's right foot buckled at a ninety-degree angle. He fell gently to the ground and assumed everything was fine, that he'd crossed the harmless threshold he read about online. But after standing, Frank discovered he couldn't feel his right foot, stiff as board. It was evening in August, and the breeze gave Frank gooseflesh, a coming attraction for the autumn to come.

Frank managed the short drive home and undid his Blazers at the door. A softball-sized lump emerged from his ankle sock, and Frank just stared at it, checking his watch to see when his mother would return from Mineo's. In high school, he'd fallen dozens of times on his cheapo skateboard from K-Mart and popped right back up like a spring. During hockey games, he must have collapsed against the unforgiving ice a hundred times and not once did he suffer an injury! How had this happened when he was skating so slowly, barely doing anything, barely even moving? He typed "swollen ankle" into his phone and elevated his leg in his father's old armchair, icing the sprain with a bag of frozen peas.

His mother found him there hours later. She listlessly said hello from the doorway, undoing her discount sneakers and setting them next to his Blazers. But when she noticed her son pressing frozen peas to his ankle, she raised her hand to her lips and asked, "What happened, Frankie? Show me."

Frank had dreaded this moment all evening but didn't see any way around it. He removed the peas, revealing the softball-shaped bulge as large and distressing as before, not black and blue or even purple, but white like a perfectly formed snowball.

"You're thirty-six years old and fooling around with skateboards! Mamma-draga, Mamma-draga."

If Frank had even a tiny bit more energy, he would've rolled his eyes. All his life his mother had invoked "Mamma-draga" after every misfortune—from the Steelers losing the opening coin toss to when she called Frankie explaining that his father had suffered a heart attack while driving. She'd discovered Mamma-draga through her grandfather, a butcher in the Strip District who emigrated from a small mountain town in Sicily. Nonno Nicola captivated Frank's mother with harrowing tales of Mamma-draga, the Sicilian ogress who terrified the island's bambini. According to him, Mamma-draga lived in a subterranean realm connected to the surface through a magical portal at the bottom of every trash bin in Sicily! All day and all night, Mamma-draga lurked, waiting for some unsuspecting child to loot around the trash, and only then would she pounce, luring the fool below with tales of *gelo di melone*. If a child was a well-behaved Catholic who had recently confessed their sins to the priest, Mamma-draga made good on her promises, and the bambino returned to the surface fruit-drunk and draped in the finest silks. But if the child hadn't confessed, Mamma-draga consumed the nasty child whole, savoring its blood the way Nonno Nicola relished his nightly glass of Chianti, the ogress decorating the underground with the shattered bones of dead children.

Frank had heard enough about Mamma-draga to last a lifetime, yet even now the ogress held power over him. His mother described Mamma-draga as a hulking grandmother with stringy white hair, and Frank still imagined her luring Pittsburgh's wicked into the underground of Sicilian legend, down through the city's trash. When his father died, that's where he pictured him—hung up on a chain dragged by Mamma-draga through a cave. Even after months and months of trying, that's where he imagined his unblossomed children—sealed away in the ruined world below.

• • •

The next morning, Frank scheduled a virtual visit with Amy's doctor who he hadn't seen in two years, not since they were trying. Dr. Fernandez occasionally accepted patients as a general practitioner but was primarily an OBGYN, and Frank had to beg to be seen, explaining that he could barely put any weight on his leg.

"This looks terrible," Dr. Fernandez announced, her face a blurry mess like an old video game. Frank held the phone to his swollen ankle and shifted awkwardly in his father's armchair. "How did you fall?" she asked.

Frank scratched his cheek and looked at the popcorn ceiling. Growing up, he had no opinions about popcorn ceilings whatsoever. The ceiling in his living room was simply an immutable fact of life, no different from the sky or the wind. But while house hunting with Amy, she turned to him in a ranch home and motioned to its identical popcorn ceiling. "It looks cheap," she told him. Frank coughed into his fist. Had Amy—who grew up in the upper-crust suburbs of Sewickley—thought this when she first met his mother, when she microwaved Italian wedding soup from Mineo's and put out the good meats and cheeses? The worst part was that now he couldn't look at his mother's popcorn ceiling without thinking "It looks cheap" either. There were shards of his ex-wife inside his body he would never extract. And the scary thing—the fear that kept him up at night—was what precisely he'd left behind in her.

"I fell while skateboarding," he finally told the doctor.

Her eyebrows arched. "Your chart says you're thirty-six."

"That's right."

"Mr. Catalano, far be it from me to tell patients what they should or should not do with their recreation time, but I'd urge you to stop skateboarding. It's not exactly friendly to the middle-aged."

Frank pinched his knee.

"The good news is there doesn't seem to be any structural damage. I'm going to send you some rehab exercises on MyChart. Otherwise, you just have to keep off it for three months."

Frank couldn't imagine being confined to his childhood bedroom for three whole months, and he just stared at the doctor, trying to think of anything at all to say. "Dr. Fernandez," he finally managed, "do you still see Amy?"

He brought the phone close to his face, but Dr. Fernandez said nothing, the silence between them thick and menacing and hot.

• • •

Fortunately for Frank, his boss at the shipping company understood about the accident. "There's no reason we need you in the office," Tamara told him happily over the phone. She emailed a link to an app, and within minutes Frank was ready to work remotely. Trader Joe's wasn't nearly as accommodating. When Frank called and explained the situation, the assistant manager—a kid who looked all of sixteen—said they had no choice but to "let him go" like he was a sickly trout.

What surprised Frank most about those first weeks of bedrest was how difficult it was to fill his days—cocooned in his childhood bedroom by all his old triumphs, the hockey trophies, his framed jersey gathering dust on the faux-wood paneling. He dozed through bowling on ESPN, skimmed an oral history of the Penguins' championship season in '92, binged the entirety of *Friday Night Lights*. Mostly, he watched YouTube on his laptop, joining Madame Genevieve's Séances live. How badly Frank had complained about his wife falling asleep every night with an iPad on her stomach, how deeply he hated the brooding figure of Madame Genevieve—shrouded in lace that concealed her face—chanting to the ghouls beyond. Each night, caller after caller dialed in, and Madame Genevieve served as their medium, allowing the bereaved to chat briefly with their dead. Amy had fallen asleep to the macabre antics of Madame Genevieve since college and had developed an interest in what Frank termed "baby witchcraft," meaning elaborate tarot card sets from eBay, visits to the local fortune teller, and winding down every night to Madame Genevieve's digital séances. Whenever Amy asked why it bothered him, Frank would mumble something inconclusive and roll on his side.

Although he never would have admitted it, Frank still couldn't shake his Catholic upbringing even though he'd stopped going to mass twenty years earlier. He attended Catholic school from kindergarten through twelfth grade and still suffered the occasional nightmare where Sister Dolores chased him through the green halls of his grade school, ruler in one hand, good book in the other. His best friend Rocco had mocked religion even back then, changing the lyrics of hymns during mass, singing, "Hail Mary, full of shit, hallowed be my cock," while Frank squirmed uncomfortably nearby, unable to ignore his fear of fire and brimstone, of being chained and beaten until the end of time, tricked into the underground by Mamma-draga. How eagerly he anticipated confession, when he would leave the priest's chamber purged of his sins, forgiven, forgiven, forgiven, a cleansing Frank still deeply craved. And yet, after the divorce, the mildly sacrilegious Madame Genevieve returned him if even briefly to the salad days of his marriage. Watching her from his twin bed in Squirrel Hill, Frank was free to analyze his divorce from a completely new viewpoint, and only then did he accept the truth: his marriage was doomed from the start.

Amy grew up in Sewickley, a rich suburb a half-hour's drive from the

Catalano side of their duplex. She studied finance and graduated magna cum laude from Pitt, while Frank barely finished community college after changing his major five times and transferring out of Duquesne. They met at a bar crawl birthday celebrating a casual acquaintance. By twenty-six, Frank was accustomed to letting women approach him, had cultivated this talent as captain of Central Catholic's hockey team. During the bar crawl, Frank noticed Amy watching him somewhere around his third Yuengling, and what initially intrigued him about her was how little she resembled the women who typically took an interest in him. No jean skirt. No Ugg boots. No North Face jacket. Frank never dated prom queens, but his girlfriends were always an integral component of the social elite. Amy dressed like a librarian in boot-cut jeans and a pilly turtleneck. She looked like a gawky nerd, and on any other night he would have ignored her. But Frank barely knew anyone on the bar crawl and felt surprisingly lonely and vulnerable.

Frank moved conveniently closer to Amy until she finally introduced herself. And after twenty minutes of banter, he wrote down her number on a napkin before walking back to his fleabag apartment in Greenfield. He didn't know if he actually wanted to call her, but his father had died a month earlier, and what he remembered most about the entire experience—not his mother's frantic call, or eating an Almond Joy in the ER, not choosing the casket from a wrinkled catalog at the funeral home, or even watching his father descend into Mamma-draga's underground—was the promise Frank made to himself after escaping his family and burying his grief in a takeout carton from New Dumpling House. He vowed to put his life in order, that he was twenty-six and the time had come to become an adult and settle down. When tickets for the Pens game fell through that weekend, Frank decided to call Amy for a date. She was friendly, intelligent, talkative, and this was enough to plan a second date, and a third, and a fourth, and before he knew it, they were dating.

Frank was drawn to her steadiness. From a young age, Amy knew she wanted to work in finance and hadn't deviated from that desire once, working even then as a consultant for a nonprofit in the Hill District. Amy—Frank guessed—admired his spontaneity and ability to go with the flow.

While she bused to the Hill District every morning for six years, Frank tried his luck as an apprentice mechanic, a manager at Jerry's Records, and an office supplies manager. Amy tunneled down, while Frank branched out, amassing a vast surface lacking depth. They joked about it at parties, their wedding, how they balanced one another.

In the quiet moments confined to his childhood bedroom, Frank wondered if their marriage fell apart not because they couldn't get pregnant but because Amy's nonprofit shuttered. Even in the darkest days of their trying—their enthusiastic sex life reduced to a rote task as romantic as a colonoscopy—they clung to the fumes of the old days, clawing for that now hidden spark of the old affection. But after the nonprofit collapsed, Amy announced her plans to transition into corporate finance, that she hoped to one day buy a McMansion in her childhood suburb of Sewickley. She was quickly hired by the largest financial firm downtown, the self-proclaimed "Ernst & Young of the 'burgh."

The change didn't come all at once, but soon enough Amy was making twice as much as Frank, then three times, then four. The pilly turtlenecks and bad jeans were replaced by a tasteful wardrobe from Brooks Brothers and longer nights at the office. Frank refused to compromise—he knew this now and regretted it and blamed his working-class upbringing and hang-ups—and sulked through wine and cheese parties with Amy's coworkers, how he balked at potential trips to the Bahamas or Europe, refusing to consider flipping their split-level for something in the wealthier suburbs closer to Amy's pregnant sister. One Saturday in their seventh year of marriage, his wife didn't come home after an evening with friends and returned the next morning explaining nothing. It happened again the next month and three times the month after that. Frank never asked about it, and finally Amy told him she wanted to provoke him by staying out all night, that she needed evidence he still loved her. He told her he didn't. It felt true in the moment.

Sometimes, his mother asked him about the divorce. She would sit on the edge of his bed and rub Frank's feet the way she did when he was sick as a child. She wanted to know what divorce felt like in his body.

"It felt," he said, leaning deeper into his pillows, "like a plane taking off. You bought the ticket. You made the decision. But once you've boarded, you can't stop it no matter how much you want to."

"You took her for granted," she told him, "like she didn't deserve you. Like you were some big shot because you were captain of the hockey team and Amy was a bookworm."

He stared at his mother but didn't hear her. Maybe divorce wasn't like a flight at all. Maybe he'd never find the right analogy. Maybe it was unnamable, untraceable, as unexplainable and mysterious as blood, the stars, the cruel passage of time.

• • •

After a month in bed, Frank made a critical discovery. If he drank two tumblers of Jack and paired it with an edible, he could numb his ankle enough so he could actually walk around. He started gingerly, rising out of bed and marching through the living room under the cheap popcorn ceiling. The next day, after a mild hangover, Frank went a step further, moving between the living room and kitchen. He always waited for his mother to go to Mineo's, and he never looked at the Crimson Cross skateboard she left to fade in the sun against the paint-peeling garage outside. He wasn't sure what to do with his newfound freedom and considered driving to Amy's new home in Sewickley. He hadn't spoken to her since he called at 1 a.m. after drinking all night at Silky's two months earlier. He'd say the same thing if he could see her now—he was lying when he claimed he didn't love her. He wished he could have given her a child and suddenly found himself desperate for her forgiveness even if he didn't understand for what or even why.

He removed the Jack from under his bed and poured himself a glass, relishing that first sip burning down his throat. He popped an edible next—how harmless, like Gushers on the playground—and stared at the popcorn ceiling, waiting for it to kick in.

Frank received the edibles when Rocco flew in from Manhattan to celebrate his divorce. His best friend had played center on the hockey team in high school, but Frank was the more driven competitor, assisting on most of his goals, covering for his shortcomings on the defensive end. Now, Rocco was a lawyer at some high-powered firm Frank always forgot the name of—WASP, WASP, and Wop, Rocco joked—and returned to Squirrel Hill in a Mercedes from the airport, handing Frank the baggie of edibles as a gift.

They drove to their old favorite, Tessaro's in Bloomfield, where they drank expensive bourbons and Frank ordered his favorite burger—how jealous Rocco looked eating his pathetic Caesar salad. They discussed high school and their playoff loss junior year, how they could've gone all the way if Billy Boy Ricci, their incompetent goalie, hadn't shit his pants in the final period against North Allegheny. They drank until last call, when finally Rocco became sullen, gathering up his courage. He'd always been like this, Frank knew. Even in high school Rocco waited till he was blackout drunk before revealing to Frankie at a bonfire that he wasn't sticking around Pittsburgh after all, that he'd decided to go to Penn State.

"Frankie." Rocco slapped his shoulder. "You gotta win Amy back."

"What the fuck, man? We just finished the divorce."

"I'm just saying, you're not doing any better than her."

What Frank remembered most vividly about his early courtship with Amy was how once, after sex, she drunkenly admitted how surprised she was that he noticed her at all. Amy had been a geek in high school and in college dated the kind of noodle-arm twerps Frank and Rocco had spent their whole lives ignoring. She never thought she would date a one-time captain of the hockey team who watched the Steelers on weekends and played in a pickup league, and this apparently gave her a little thrill. When Frank mentioned this years later, Amy told him to never bring it up again, that it was the pathetic ramblings of a drunken child. But Frank didn't think it was pathetic at all. It was the essential thread that drew them together. She saw him in his best possible light.

"She was lucky to marry me," Frank told Rocco.

Rocco laughed so hard he had to set down his glass. "Bro, that's your problem. You always condescended to her. She's this super smart finance chick who knows stuff about French food, and you're this fucking guinea from Squirrel Hill reminiscing about Catholic school hockey games from twenty years ago. You don't want to be out here, my dude." He gestured to the crowd who had willingly gathered at Tessaro's for last call. "It blows ass out here."

Frank lay in bed and finished his glass of Jack before pouring himself another, aware of how badly he needed purpose and some vague and all-encompassing forgiveness. He'd fallen into the habit of watching Madame Genevieve five or six hours each night. She summoned a viewer's wife from the dead in stunning 4K and suddenly Frank knew what he had to do. He could simply call Genevieve and beg for help! Sure, Amy wasn't dead, and he had no interest in hearing from his father, but even the illusion of chatting with his wife again might be enough to calm his rattled nerves, to free him from the desire to actually speak with her, to put things straight when they were by all accounts irreparable. Maybe she was watching in Sewickley. Maybe she would hear him. Frank's heart thudded against the meat of his chest, and before he could change his mind, he typed in MadameGenevieve.com on his laptop.

Viewers who wanted to interact with the Madame simply logged into her website and Venmoed $100. When their turn rolled around, their mic went live on YouTube. Onscreen, Madame Genevieve sat by a cheap table and candelabra, tarot cards and an honest-to-goodness crystal ball. She always wore a lace cloak that covered her eyes, making it impossible to see her face. But from her painted lips and syrupy voice, Frank assumed she was around his age, the grown-up version of the goth posers at Central Catholic who loved Depeche Mode and Garbage. When Amy first introduced Frank to her videos, he assumed everyone knew Madame Genevieve was a fake. But over the years, he'd witnessed the YouTube medium relay information impossible to guess—birthdates, the placement of unusual scars, the itinerary of cruises taken decades ago. Frank figured these mourners were plants meant to sucker in fools, but he suddenly wanted to believe.

BlackAndGold1984_Guy appeared on a six-name waiting list, and an admin PMed Frank, reminding him to gather two talismans familiar to the dead. He'd forgotten all about this and quickly scanned his bedroom, finding nothing that reminded him of Amy. But he couldn't afford to flush a hundred bucks down the toilet, so he chugged his Jack, swung his legs off the bed, and began searching for some trinket that evoked his ex-wife. He limped into the kitchen and saw his skateboard propped up outside against his father's ruined garage.

Frank stepped outside for the first time in weeks, and it felt like crossing into a new and different world. He couldn't articulate it, but the stars in the sky didn't feel the same. It wasn't the sky he recognized from childhood or even from a few months earlier. The moon hung slightly crooked, everything just an inch off.

In this new and peculiar landscape, Frank saw himself clearly for perhaps the first time since he was a teenager. He still viewed the world through the lenses he established in high school and judged other people purely on their appearance or physical prowess. It was a shallow value system, and he understood this was because at his core he remained a shallow person, drifting through life without intentionality, squandering his days on whatever fleeting attraction caught his eye. He had burned through years of his life and punished his ex-wife for recognizing this and restarting hers. Tears welled in his eyes for the first time since childhood, and Frank was terrified that he would never grow or change, that his faults possessed their own gravity that would tether him until the day he died and returned to the soil. He told himself this wasn't true. He was still a young man after all. He was still so young.

Frank approached his father's garage, and even this looked wrong somehow, too wobbly and full. His skateboard—the one thing he recognized from the old world—was still leaning against the siding where his mother left it, but it seemed to Frank that the board was holding up the shack and not vice versa. Look, I want to be clear here. These visions, sensations, however you want to define them, were not the product of Rocco's cheap edibles from Manhattan. These were birthed someplace else, somewhere hidden deep underground.

Frank limped to the skateboard and pulled it loose. Neither the world nor the garage collapsed, and he felt grateful for the first time in months. He returned to bed and balanced the board between his face and the glowing screen, the bloody cross and ghosts staring up at him. He swallowed his saliva and twisted off his wedding band, setting it gingerly on the board. Then his computer beeped, and a message told him he was going live in five, four, three, two, one . . .

"Greetings, Black and Gold 1984 Guy. It is I, Madame Genevieve, dark witch arcana of the grand beyond! Who do you seek on this fine autumn evening, my love?"

Three thousand people were watching, and comments raced up the screen. GET ON WITH IT, LETS GOOOO, MORE GHOSTZ PLZ. Frank clutched his bedsheets and said, "Hi."

Madame Genevieve nodded ever so slightly. "Ciao. I ask again—who do you wish to speak to, Mr. Black and Gold?"

Sweat pooled along Frank's back, and he worried they could see him somehow, shirtless and incapacitated in his childhood bedroom, surrounded by what remained of his teenage potential. "Amy," he whispered.

The shrouded medium wrote her name with a quill. "And what was your relationship with this Amy?"

"She was my wife."

A fresh stream of comments: SO SORRY, OH NO, RIP AMY!

"The mistress macabre is sorry for your loss." She waved her hands through bits of smoke curling up from her incense. "Shall we begin?"

"I'm ready," Frank said.

Madame Genevieve's lips fluttered, business as usual so far. "Mr. Black and Gold," she whispered. "I've now entered the spirit realm and have come across an othersider with ferocious energy. Are you holding Amy's talismans? Don't let them go."

The comments multiplied—OH SHIT, HERE WE GO, CHAT UP THAT GHOST GEN—as Frank rubbed his wedding ring in little circles over the skateboard.

"Amy's spirit beckons," Genevieve announced, her voice an octave lower now. "May I allow the deceased to speak?"

Frank leaned closer. "Please."

She tilted her head. Canned thunder exploded offscreen. "Beloved, I have returned. It's your lovely Amy."

FUCK, GET HIM AMY, #AMY4LYFE

"Hi," Frank managed.

Madame Genevieve jerked to the right. Everything in her room turned white. "Why did you summon me, bridegroom?"

"Amy," Frank said, hoping his wife was really watching, "I just want you to know that I'm sorry. I took you for granted, I was intimidated by you, and I've lived a shallow life." He scratched his jaw. It was impossible articulating the truth he'd come to in the backyard, and he knew his words lacked conviction. "I'm just really sorry for the person I've been. I apologize for being me."

And then something happened that Frank Catalano had never seen during his many years watching Madame Genevieve. The medium slumped back in her chair, breathing quickly now, spit running down cracked lips. Her left hand rose slowly, shaking, until at last she reached her veil and pinched it between trembling index finger and thumb. She tore the garment from her body, and at last Madame Genevieve was revealed. All this time Frank had been wrong. The YouTuber was no media-savvy millennial, milking the mourning of their money. Madame Genevieve looked older than Frank's mother, older than all those nuns who terrified him in his youth, older than the grandmother who died when Frank was just a child. She looked ancient, risen from the underground, hair as white as snow, eyes rolled back into her head showing only the red-speckled whites. Madame Genevieve convulsed as she moved her right hand over the incense flame, allowing her paper skin to catch fire and burn. "I do not forgive you, Frank," she screamed before the video went dead, forever and ever, amen.

The Faith Center

My wife and I couldn't find the entrance to the Faith Center. We'd walked a mile from the Manzoni metro stop amid the heat of late August, and already I'd sweated through my shirt, my sport coat draped over my shoulder in a heap. My wife, ever the solver, flagged down a carabiniere and in her rudimentary Italian asked, *"Scusa, signor? Dov'e il Faith Center?"* But he just shrugged, and we wandered the perimeter of a walled park until at last I saw them in the distance, silhouetted by the beating sun—my students, the telltale signs of American youth, in T-shirts and shorts looking so different from the Italians they had flown across the globe to supposedly meet. Their European counterparts dressed in uniform—men in blue suits, polished shoes; women in dark jeans, leather jackets—and this underscored how young our students looked in comparison. I was only fifteen years their senior, my wife just ten, yet they still felt like the children we had no intentions of having, smiling good-natured babies.

"Hi, Michael!" one of them shouted. "Hi, Michael!" came another, then another, then another, then similar greetings for my wife. I didn't mind their informality and actually encouraged it. But as the chain of thirty students approached, I noticed the surprised look of the middle-aged woman leading them. Silver-haired and confident in clothes that were so plain they were almost attention-grabbing, she reminded me of all those grizzled nuns of my youth, those put-upon women who lorded over my Catholic school in dead-end Scranton. Dimitris, the Rome Innovation Campus Director, had told me a little about her—Dr. Claire Logan, an Irish professor of Catholic Studies who directed the Faith Center and was teaching our students Global Christianity. Outside of funerals, I hadn't been inside a church since my teens and had no idea what a student learned in a class like Global Christianity, but it sounded like torture to me.

"Professor Mancuso," she said, as Jean and I fell in line, "I'm so thankful to have this opportunity to meet you and your lovely wife. We're just so blessed to have you."

She said this like someone who didn't believe it in the slightest. There was a sarcastic lilt in her voice, and I could tell by her eyes that she was shocked we looked so young. I was perpetually baby-faced even as I approached forty, and I'd long ago made peace with being confused for a student again and again no matter how many ties and jackets I added to my wardrobe. Those days were drawing to their end, and I was trying desperately to enjoy them. "Yeah," I managed. "Totally."

Technically, I was Dr. Logan's supervisor for the semester. The home campus had chosen me to serve as that year's Academic Director of Rome Innovation which meant that in addition to living with students in Italy for three months while teaching Introduction to Italian Cinema, I was also expected to evaluate the adjuncts abroad and make sure everything was up to Minnesotan standards. It was Dimitris who insisted I attend the first Faith Center Emergence Dinner of the year, Dimitris who with a wry smile said I'd just adore the scintillating conversation. Dr. Logan knew this and didn't comment on it, but who wouldn't resent being assessed by someone three decades her junior?

She led our parade of loud, gangly Americans around and around the marble enclosure of the Faith Center until at last she came to a small box attached to the wall. She pressed a button, and a small keypad and speaker were revealed. We watched her tap three numbers summoning the front desk, and I stared at Jean and wanted to ask how we would've gotten inside if we hadn't stumbled upon Dr. Logan.

The Faith Center was a series of plain academic buildings surrounded by trees and impressive greenery, marble busts of various saints, a functional chicken coop, and wandering paths where legions of cats roamed free, meowing and stretching in patches of sunlight. Dr. Logan steered us up a hill that overlooked the Coliseum, and even I, someone who crossed the street if I happened upon a priest at night, had to admit it was all somewhat moving. But the students were forever students, squealing over the animals and taking selfies with cats, completely ignoring the view that so few had ever enjoyed. I tried prodding them to the overlook, but Dr. Logan whisked us away. "There's no time," she said. "We have a busy, and might I add rewarding, night ahead."

We entered a narrow hallway lined with preppy twenty-somethings who literally clapped upon our arrival. I vaguely understood that the Faith Center was an international gathering place for people who wanted to study Christianity a mere three miles from the Vatican. So maybe these were students? Graduate students of some kind? Back on the home campus, the Associate Vice Provost for Global Learning and Strategy assured me that I wouldn't have to do anything in Rome that made me uncomfortable, that I could skip trips to the Vatican or various churches or really anything that might ignite my anxiety. But when we walked into the cafeteria swarmed with clergy and nuns, I understood that this would be an exceedingly difficult evening. Dr. Logan told the students to find a seat, to mix in with the priests and nuns and strike up a conversation about this evening's topic—vocation apparently.

I excused myself to the men's room and locked myself inside a stall. Then I removed the small vial of Propranolol I kept on my person at all times. It's funny, because my primary care physician prescribed me 20 mg of Propranolol a whole year before I saw a therapist and was informed that I'd been wrestling with PTSD for close to two decades. The Propranolol slowed my heart rate and could sometimes halt or even prevent a panic attack, but my therapist, a boomer in the habit of playing sixties protest songs at the beginning and end of each session, was skeptical of the pill's effectiveness. According to Dr. Jones, the only path forward was a biweekly dose of sessions coupled with daily meditation and books on mindfulness by writers I'd never heard of like Jon Kabat-Zinn and Pema Chödrön. When I told him that I'd already committed to leaving the country for ninety days, he frowned and asked, "Bring me back a pizza, paisan?"

I pooled saliva in my cheek and swallowed one of the powder blue pills. When I was eighteen in my final year of Catholic school, my best friend came out to me and I did not handle it well. He was a willowy, sweet kid, former altar boy, deeply religious like the rest of us poor kids in Scranton. Two weeks after he told me, Keith shot himself in his attic, and then I went off to college six hours away and told no one—and I mean no one—what happened. That regret, that guilt, that denial had calcified into PTSD, a condition I'd tried for years to erase with booze, movies, exercise, anything that briefly lifted me from the shell of my body. When Dr. Jones explained this, my first instinct was to apologize. How could I have PTSD when I hadn't even served? But Dr. Jones assured me it was more common than I thought, and the two of us were still in the early stages of pinpointing my triggers and how to effectively deal with them. Catholicism, however, was one of the big ones, all the reminders of what had shaped both my reaction to Keith's coming out and his eventual suicide. I felt marked by death and irredeemable, common responses Dr. Jones explained over a Bob Dylan song.

Everyone had already taken their seats in the cafeteria when I returned, the students gulping wine as priests and nuns lectured them. I scanned the room for my wife and found Jean in the corner, surrounded by our most timid and awkward students who sought her out like moths to a light. She caught my gaze and gave me this apologizing look, and I tried to signal her not to worry, that this wasn't her fault. She was the one who had helped me seek out Dr. Jones, the one who stroked my hair while I drunkenly told her about Keith over and over, retraumatizing myself I learned later. She was my anchor, my tether to the world, and I understood that she'd sacrificed by coming to Rome, that the powers-that-be at her job—a high-level marketing firm in the tallest skyscraper of Minneapolis—weren't exactly thrilled that she'd be working remotely for three whole months. I tried smiling at her, but Jean saw right through me.

Instead, it was Dr. Logan who'd made sure to save me a seat, Dr. Logan who grabbed my elbow and said, "We've been waiting for you."

Only three students were sitting at her table. They rarely wanted to eat with the adults, and who could blame them? Instead, Dr. Logan guided me toward members of the clergy and the graduate students who hadn't touched a drop of their wine. She introduced us and maintained eye contact with me for an uncomfortable length of time. "We really missed you, Professor Mancuso, at the Vatican Museums tour. I do hope you get a chance to visit sooner rather than later. You just have to attend mass at St. Peter's, although I actually prefer Chiesa di Santa Maria off Piazza di San Bernardo. There's a spectacular Bernini inside. *The Ecstasy of Teresa*? Have you been?"

While Dr. Logan led students through a multi-hour exploration of the Vatican Museums, I'd taken tram 19 to VIGAMUS, Rome's extremely sad video game museum which was essentially just a basement housing a few old arcade games and plaster statues of characters I vaguely remembered from the nineties. "No, I haven't been," I told her.

A priest frowned. "Hmm," he said. "What's your favorite church in Rome then?"

I took a long sip of wine and thought about saying VIGAMUS. "I'm not sure yet?"

Dr. Logan tilted her head. "You must be jet-lagged."

We'd arrived nine days earlier. "Yes. I'm extremely jet-lagged."

She checked her watch before clinking her fork against her glass. It must be said that Dr. Logan did not strike me as a bad person whatsoever. It made sense that she assumed the Academic Director of Rome Innovation would have some modicum of interest in the Vatican and Catholicism or at the very least would fake it as a model for their students. I was the one in the wrong. Like always, I felt out of place, that I needed to justify why I was here, there, anywhere.

"I can't express how happy I am to see you all here tonight," Dr. Logan said after moving to a podium at the front of the room.

I watched my students shift awkwardly in their seats. I'd only met them a few times in the run-up to Rome and was still trying to memorize their names. Half of them looked wine-buzzed and, after a day of touring religious sites with Dr. Logan, would probably struggle staying awake. But some looked rapt with attention, sitting with perfect posture, the kind of students who'd gravitated to Rome Innovation because of the implied religious content, churchy kids in long skirts and too big dress shirts that reminded me of the nerdiest nerds from my high school.

But then my gaze fell on Harrison in the back. He looked absurdly lanky even sitting down and wore the same outfit every day—ripped denim shorts, unlaced Air Jordans, and a deep v-neck tee. His hair was dyed platinum blond, and it was obvious to everyone that he was the social fulcrum of our trip. Every student adored him, and his loud voice echoed down the halls of our dorm, his name semi-permanent in the WhatsApp chat Dimitris insisted we join, Jean included. Harrison's messages were a flood of emojis and GIFs from TV shows I'd never heard of, and he proudly talked about both his queerness and desire to meet a "beautiful but extremely intelligent Italian gentleman, someone who can cook and is hopefully depressed but not too depressed. A vegan maybe?" My therapist had already identified that I felt overly protective of my LGBTQ+ students and needed to stop, that I was projecting, that they certainly didn't need my protection unless they specifically asked for it which few rarely did. But I couldn't help but observe Harrison in this environment, surrounded by priests and nuns, listening to Dr. Logan explain the ins and outs of modern vocation. He didn't appear anxious or even defiant. He just seemed bored, fingering a hole in his shorts. I watched him and tried to prevent myself from disassociating. I dug my fingernails into my knees and knew Dr. Jones didn't particularly approve of this coping method.

A man emerged from the back of the cafeteria, waving his hand, and wordlessly the grad students followed him out. A moment later, they returned balancing plates of food like well-trained waiters. Why Dr. Logan continued talking, I didn't know, because each and every one of our undergrads turned to the food, oblivious to whatever she was saying. I felt grateful for the distraction, and when I received my plate of ragu with its plain little side salad, I immediately plunged a fork into an al dente tube of pasta and brought it to my lips. The priest across from me—Antonio he'd explained—shook his head before I realized that of course we were expected to say grace. Of course!

Dr. Logan bowed her head, and again I tried to ignore her, to imagine a movie playing in my head. The next day, Jean and I planned to visit Cinecittà—Rome's equivalent of Hollywood with a museum attached to the backlot. I tried picturing the two of us walking hand-in-hand under a clear blue sky surrounded by the ghosts of Fellini, Marciano, Antonioni. But even this couldn't calm me, and when Dr. Logan implored us to *mangia, mangia*, I felt my heartbeat thudding in my eardrums, winning the battle against Propranolol in real time.

Sweat pooled on my back and I knew I needed to remove my jacket, but even that felt impossible, a herculean task that might take months, years, a lifetime. I breathed through my mouth hopeful that no one was paying attention, that the students and clergy were either too focused on the food or Dr. Logan. I tried to meditate, to enter a state of mindfulness, to imagine a literal thread running from my head to my feet, to focus on my breathing and pretend it was a ship navigating calm waters. But nothing worked, and I kept drifting back to Dr. Logan over and over.

"I'm so thrilled to introduce our first speaker today. For Christians, vocation can be broken up into three tracks—religious life, single life, and married life. We're going to hear some brilliant takes tonight by folks who are actually walking those paths, and I can't wait to hear how you all respond. First up, I'd like to introduce Mrs. Amara Rossi, a lawyer in Tivoli, a fiercely devout Catholic, and, most importantly for our purposes here tonight, a happily married woman."

A woman at the end of my table stood up and smiled. She looked about my age, but everything about her seemed more adult and confident. This was a truth impossible to ignore about the Italians. When I pictured myself or my friends back home, we all felt like overgrown kids. Sure, many of them had high-paying jobs or even children, but they routinely wore T-shirts and jeans, played Xbox, and lined up at the cinema to watch whatever billion-dollar superhero film was all the rage that month. Amara Rossi in her impeccably tailored pantsuit and heels looked like an adult from another generation, not an Italian American millennial like me, but someone who had truly experienced the world and wanted to share her hard-earned knowledge. She walked to the podium, all sophistication and class, and my familiar impostor syndrome rose out of my chest. I didn't belong there. How dare I think I deserved ninety days in Italy teaching students. How dare I.

"Ciao," Amara Rossi said. "You'll all have to forgive my English. It's absolutely dreadful." Like every Italian we'd met who said this, her English was flawless. "Marriage," she said, voice an octave deeper, "is no easy road. It might be at the beginning when everything's a honeymoon, but that feeling never lasts. It can't. It wouldn't be natural if it did."

I tried to catch Jean's attention from across the room—like everyone else, we believed our love was different from other people's, singular and superior—but her eyes were trained on Rossi.

"But whenever I falter, I think of Christ. Imagine him. Really picture him. At the end of his life, shouldering that cross, how heavy that burden must have felt. He opted into his own death for each of us. He knew he would die but followed his chosen path anyway."

I was breathing faster now, and Father Antonio noticed and studied me from the corner of his eye. I wanted so badly to pop another Propranolol, but I refused to give him the satisfaction.

"You know," Amara continued, "it's becoming very in vogue here in Rome and around the world to rethink marriage, to wonder if maybe this monumental sacrament is for everyone. A man and another man. A woman and another woman. What's next?" she asked before a light laugh. "It's not really to me to judge, but it's important for us to remember that god hasn't left us here without guidance, that we do in fact have a manual." She smiled wide. "It's called the Bible, and there are very clear and deliberate rules."

Back on the sleepy home campus, a speech like this would cause an uproar. Our students had self-selected into a small liberal arts college in the upper Midwest, and the kids expected the administration to combat microaggressions and bigotry even if they did so in halfhearted, neoliberal ways. There was obviously a gap between the home campus and whatever Dr. Logan was staging here in the Faith Center, and that would fall to me to correct, a conversation I was already dreading. I sought out Harrison and was surprised to find him seemingly unfazed. He shoveled the last bits of pasta into his mouth, then filled his glass of wine. Harrison just seemed so serene, so above it all, and I found myself jealous, breathing through my mouth, clutching my knees, wondering if my friend Keith could have survived this dinner as unscathed as my students.

• • •

Amara Rossi was followed by Giordano—a single man who dedicated every waking moment to a soup kitchen slowly being priced out of nearby Trastevere—who was followed by Sister Raymond O'Sullivan—a self-proclaimed "super nun" who claimed to rescue sex trafficked women, walking bravely into Neapolitan brothels and offering a hand to anyone willing to follow her back to the convent. My body flooded with adrenaline, and eventually I settled into my perpetual fear-state, a deep and tangible paranoia. It felt like tumbling through a sheet of ice into a new world where anything was possible, where I might finally access some darker or primordial version of myself, the mask of identity I presented to the world at last stripped away, revealing the maw at the cratered center of my personality.

I drank a third glass of wine and told myself these were not evil people, that Amara Rossi's homophobia notwithstanding, each of them contributed good to the world, that the problem was me and me alone. I was the only one uncomfortable here, not my wife, not even my students. Dr. Logan asked us to utilize our after-dinner hour as an opportunity to discuss what we'd heard and engage one-one-one with the speakers. Predictably, the students clustered around Harrison who monologued about his weekend plans—an AirBnB in Florence!—while the adults defected one-by-one to my table, all save for Jean pinned down by the same group of students from earlier.

"May I join you?"

I looked up and saw Amara Rossi, smiling, friendly, unexpectedly tall.

"Sure."

She held a plastic cup of panna cotta, completely untouched. "Dr. Logan says you're running Rome Innovation this year. That's such a wonderful opportunity. I speak with these students every year, and they're always such a fascinating bunch. They're so studious!"

I glanced back at Harrison who was loudly explaining why the tequila sunrise was scientifically the best cocktail. "They really are," I said.

I tried confining our conversation to small talk—what are your favorite restaurants, what's the most must-see museum in Rome—but slowly and surely more of the Faith Center regulars glommed onto our conversation. Dr. Logan, Nunzio Giordano, two of the graduate students, even Father Antonio. Amara was describing the church where she'd been married five years earlier, an extremely personal site, she explained, that represented everything good and pure in Italy, a breathtaking architectural marvel that stood shoulder-to-shoulder with the Trevi Fountain or the Spanish Steps if only the tourists could really and truly see it.

"What church were you married in?" Dr. Logan asked me.

"Yes," Amara said, "please, tell us. American churches are so particular."

My wife and I had been married in an antique museum beneath a rusted-out boat. Her lesbian aunt presided over the event, and I walked out with my best men to an eighties pro wrestling entrance song. I looked at Dr. Logan and knew it was horrible, but I wanted to wound her, badly. I was sweaty and tired and angry and confused. I wanted to explode.

"We weren't married in a church," I said. "We . . ." I closed my eyes and tried to imagine the exact string of words that could convey everything I had held so tightly for so long. I wanted to tell them that I didn't believe in any of this, that they were wasting not only each other's time, but the students' and mine as well. I wanted to tell them that I hated them, everyone who so easily believed, everyone who tossed out laws and dogma like a comforting shawl, oblivious to the consequences, to my best friend climbing into his attic with a shotgun cradled to his chest, the determination and shame our upbringing had instilled. I wanted to blame them, each and every one, but like always my anger deflated like a slashed tire. I would never be the type of man who exploded. I would always turn it inward and implode. Everything had been my fault, all of it, and if only I had behaved better, had said something positive to Keith, had not suggested he hide what was so obvious to everyone in our bullshit town, then maybe, just maybe he would still be here. He could be in Rome or Scranton or anywhere really, alive. Alive.

Amara Rossi leaned forward. "Perhaps I'm not following you? Maybe it's my English."

I looked at all those moon-blank faces. I felt very far away from myself, watching events from a great and peaceful distance. "The problem is I'm not supposed to be here," I told them. "I'm the one who should've died."

• • •

Twenty years earlier, Keith and I lay sprawled on the roof of his parents' garage. It was the August before our senior year, and we'd just returned from Wilkes-Barre following a punk show at Café Metropolis, the shady all-ages club. The performance itself was fine—headlined by some Marywood kids calling themselves Throat Punch Tim Allen—and now we were smoking a Swisher Sweet Keith liberated from his older brother's bedroom. He thought it might be laced with weed, but I didn't feel much staring at the velvety stars, the skyline of Scranton unfurled before us, the neon Electric City sign blinking out an SOS to the wider world. But Keith insisted he was high, that he felt different, fresh, reborn. I passed him the cigar and was overcome by the same melancholia that so many teens from Rust Belt nowheres must experience—the prickling sensation like a limb fallen asleep that I would never leave this place, that Scranton was as permanent as my circumstances, that I would always and forever haunt these streets above abandoned coal mines, searching for punk shows, weed, anything with the capacity to numb. It was a fear I probed often, the scab hardening into something peculiar and powerful.

"Hey," Keith whispered through a giggle, wanting desperately to believe he was high. "Do you think we'll always be friends? Like fifty years from now or whatever?"

He was invisible beneath the moonglow save for the orange embers of his lit cigar. I didn't have to search for my answer, because it was a calculation I'd run countless times in my head. I barely knew anyone who had ever left. The chances of one person leaving were low, the chances of two people who were best friends escaping were essentially zero. I turned to Keith then—still laughing, so blissfully unaware of the tragedy yet to come—and told him "No, no, I don't think so, no."

Zeitgeist Comics, 1946

Two days shy of the collapse, I met Valerie St. James, a very different kind of gal from all the dour darlings I'd known back in Edison. Vincent's was hopping that night, the jukebox cranked loud, the ad men trading dances with a gaggle of girls rumored to be Rockettes. Dick Arnold and I watched from the sidelines trying to dream up the kind of surefire concept that might save Zeitgeist Comics and, by extension, ourselves. It was 1946, and everybody was back. You could feel it pulsing in the streets. The pants were bigger, the dresses looser, we Americans newly puffed up with the knowledge that when the big bad creepies howled from beyond the oceans, we rose up and smacked those donkeys back from which they came. Everyone looked thrilled save for Dick Arnold, the glummest artist this side of Munch's *Scream*. He was fifteen years my senior with hands as cracked as my father's. I yapped and yapped and yapped and still Dick Arnold's flat expression remained unchanged.

"And then I humped my bar gun over that lousy Kraut hill and came twenty yards—no, ten!—back from some ragtag SS SOBs about to gun down the squadron of yours truly. Not with Private Christopher Giordano on the job, no sir! I sent those schnitzel-eating Nancy's back to hell, you can be sure of that, Dick."

Dick blinked the slowest blink I'd ever seen. I spent WW2 penning training manuals in Fort Benning, Georgia, but I told war stories all the time.

My sleek Manhattanite image required it—nay, gentle reader, demanded it! And I intended to strut across the earth as a beloved, larger-than-life king.

"Uh huh," Dick said. "Let's get back to the book. I'll work on some designs this week, but be straight with me, how bad is it at Zeitgeist?"

I fingered my lip. It was a childish tic fit for a teenager, and I was doing everything I could to overcome the damn thing. Zeitgeist Comic sales had plummeted thanks to the recent surge in anti-comic sentiment, the crazy notion that funny books were somehow corrupting the nation's youth. I stared hard into Dick's eyes and couldn't fathom how anyone might gaze upon our four-color worlds of wonder and joy and not be moved by the audacity of the human spirit, the vast potential of the creative mind and what might be accomplished by the tandem of writing and art. The truth was it was only a matter of time before the division was axed. Unless, I wanted to say, unless we developed an idea so superb, so unstoppable that it salvaged the entire medium.

"The truth," I said, "is that everything's going to be fine because Christopher Giordano and Dick Arnold are on the case." I made my fingers into a movie screen and framed Dick's face. "Now picture this. We open on a down-and-out family on the outskirts of—"

But before I could unleash what surely would've been the finest idea ever hatched in Vincent's on Madison, a woman walked in with the hands of a mighty god. They were long, delicate, pristine, devoid of the everyday imperfections—moles, a stray hair, a joint jutting off course—that plagued the rest of us unwashed mortals. She had the type of hands that looked like they might reach down from the muddy skies of Edison, New Jersey, and shield me from that backwards burg forever and ever. Her powerful mitts swayed like well-timed machinery as she parted the red sea of Rockettes and sat next to me at the bar. Me! Lucky old Christopher, dastardly rascal extraordinaire.

"A sidecar," she told the bartender in a British accent that signaled two very crucial points: 1) Here was a gal made flesh from all the foreign fantasies I'd conjured in bars and automats across the great concrete island of Manhattan, and 2) This was a voice diametrically opposed to all I'd known in Edison, all those brick-heavy Italian/Polish/German accents that still allowed words of their mother tongue to slip through the red, white, and blue.

"So, your idea," Dick Arnold said, his voice like day-old chuck meat.

"Pipe down," I whispered, before turning to our new potential companion. "A sidecar, huh? Conrad here makes a pretty good one, but the best sidecar I ever had was made for me by a man named Jerry in the far-off land of Berlin."

She eyed me suspiciously over her glass. "That so?"

"Sure. Name's Christopher Giordano."

"Valerie St. James."

I'm not sure whether this next part is true, but I vaguely recall Dick Arnold groaning. Either way, his displeasure was clear from the creased lines in his forehead. Dick despised Vincent's on Madison and preferred Chumley's down the back alley by the ferry, the kind of place where day laborers ordered Schlitz and showered the hardwood with broken peanut shells. I'd been to my fair share of Chumley knockoffs and much preferred Vincent's, a bar where everyone wore suits, where everyone's face glowed with the promise of money and stature, either attained or just 'round the bend.

"This is my associate, Dick Arnold," I said with a showy wave. "Dick here is the best funny book artist in the comics biz. *Love Story. Zap. The Tomb of the Living Vampire*. All from Zeitgeist Comics where I serve the humble reading populace as Assistant Editor."

Valerie St. James leaned on her elbows. "That," she said slowly, "sounds really, really sad."

Dick Arnold burst out laughing, and what choice did I have but to release a mighty guffaw as well? I thumbed the edge of my beer glass and tried not to reveal my damaged pride. Zeitgeist Comics felt like home to me, and I thought of the forty-two souls who toiled there for the greater good of the comic-reading public as my family. "All right, Miss St. James," I said, "what do you do for a living then?"

She took a long, thoughtful sip from her sidecar. "I'm a hand model for glove advertisements with Majesty Modeling."

A hand model! For glove advertisements! What feat of altruism had I accomplished in some previous life to earn an audience with the supple British digits of Valerie St. James? Dick Arnold laughed and left a crisp Washington for his tab. He knew the score. He had a wife and daughter out in Teaneck and always left Vincent's early.

"Pleasure, Miss St. James," he said. "I'll have designs for you Thursday, Giordano."

I shooed Dick away like a mosquito. "A hand model," I said to Valerie. "That sounds exciting."

"It isn't." She downed her sidecar and signaled the bartender for a second. "I only took it because I wanted to move to Manhattan, but the truth is Manhattan is just like everywhere else. All I want to do is smoke cigars and boss people around. If I were a man, I'd become an executive."

I nodded. I was used to these kinds of quick confessionals from women, how happily they opened up for me. I'd always been approachable dating back to my tender days as a professional lunk-head at John P. Stevens High. I obliquely understood there was something vaguely romantic yet endlessly nonthreatening about my upbeat temperament and perpetually boyish face.

"The only executive I know is my boss Benson McCrae," I said. "He's sweaty as an ox and without a doubt the unhappiest hombre I've ever met. I'd venture to guess that professional hand model is a pretty good alternative."

"Maybe you're right. You said you're an assistant editor? What's that like? Where'd you go to school?"

"Princeton."

I'd visited the city of Princeton once or twice and knew just enough to make my lies plausible if push came to shove.

"Princeton? Then that's the most boring thing about you, Mr.—what did you say your name was again?"

"Giordano. Christopher Giordano." I snapped at the bartender. "Another sidecar for my lady friend, and a Manhattan for me, bub. And make 'em spicy!"

The ad men and the Rockettes played "It's Been a Long, Long Time" on the jukebox, and Valerie and I joked for the next twenty-five minutes. She told me about her frustrations with the various opportunities provided to her, her childhood in London, her subsequent exodus to the Stars and Stripes following the conclusion of World War II. I expounded on the various follies of the Merry Bullpen of Zeitgeist Comics, not to mention a totally fabricated backstory that replaced my tanning factory father in Edison with a rich but distant automobile executive hailing from a large estate in Princeton Borough. And when the tastemakers cut with the corny stuff for the fast-paced and eminently danceable "Doctor, Lawyer, Indian Chief," I invited my new acquaintance to the dance floor, and together we Lindy Hopped every which way, our limbs possessed by the faux-innocent charm of one Miss Betty Hutton. I took Valerie's hand—my body confident with alcohol—and asked for her number. "Hmm. Close, but maybe next time." And even that couldn't bring me down. Because I knew as surely as I felt the gentle curve of Valerie's hips that this was one British hand model I would definitely see again.

• • •

Zeitgeist Publishing occupied four floors of a skyscraper, a few blocks from Vincent's. The comics division had the seventh to itself, and I could barely contain my grin as the elevator doors peeled open the next morning. Our floor was a sea of ringing telephones, singing typewriters, the steady music of pencils dragged across sketch paper. We were a mishmash of secretaries, writers, artists, a small handful of junior editors. Only bigwigs like Dick Arnold who'd been there for years worked from home. I marched through the office greeting everyone I saw—Hullo, Sally; Hullo, Joe; Hullo, Paulie! And I was so moved by the sight of the nameplate on my office door that I opened my briefcase right then and there. I retrieved my trusty flute—my mother called it her piccolo and taught me to play as a boy—and held it above my head for all the gentle souls of the Merry Bullpen—a phrase I coined—to see.

"Heya, maniacs. Here's a little music to start your day off right. This one's an old Italian folk tune." I fingered my flute and provided the Bullpen with a whimsical dago ditty, the likes of which they'd never experienced before. They hooted and hollered. They stomped their feet. Epson Gerber—a journeyman artist on *Uncle Cowboy*—thrust his mug in the air and yelled hee-haw. I'd worked there six months, and in the Merry Bullpen of Zeitgeist Comics felt loved, welcomed, and accepted. And no face shone brighter than Jean Fanning, my secretary, a lanky gal whose laugh and demure forehead reminded me of my kid sister, Angela.

Jean smacked her gum. "Christopher Giordano," she said, "you are, without a doubt, the saltiest ham I ever met in my life."

I set a palm on her desk and grinned. I was only four years older than her at the wise age of twenty-three, but even then I was aware of my desire to shield Jean from the many injustices of the adult world. "Sweetie Jeanie, you look lovely today. And intelligent. And mighty. And strong. Do me a favor and call me on the intercom in oh, let's say thirty seconds. I've got some work that needs doing!"

Jean nodded, and I had no doubt whatsoever that soon she'd be an assistant editor herself, that in a few years' time she'd rule the hallowed halls of Zeitgeist Publishing like a mad titan straight out of Dick Arnold's funny books. She looked up and said, "Sure, Christopher. But your father called again. When are you going to call him back?"

My father had been calling Zeitgeist every day for the past month. He didn't have the number to my apartment in Hoboken and must have looked up Zeitgeist in the book. "Thanks," I said quietly, before slipping inside my office.

Other than the respect and camaraderie of my fellow employees, the view from my office was one of the major draws of working at Zeitgeist. It overlooked the grand buildings along Fifth Avenue, the rolling green majesty of Central Park, and even my lonely rented room across the blue waters of the Hudson. It was a view that for all intents and purposes should not have been afforded to the son of an Italian immigrant, and its existence proved that in America, all things were possible. In America, I could pen one masterful training manual after another in the sweltering humidity of Georgia and return to Manhattan as a prince and world-beating hero. It was tangible proof of all the glory yet to come.

And yet, I sank into my chair and felt pangs of envy. I wasn't wholly committed to the life of the editor, of someone who would be discarded by history. I wanted to be out there, in the Bullpen proper, weaving the kind of modern fairy tales Zeitgeist Comics buttered its toast with. My boss, Benson McCrae, begrudgingly allowed me to write three-page prose stories about jilted brides and cuckolded husbands that appeared in the final pages of *Love Story,* but my real duties boiled down to paper pushing, to assigning books to artists like Dick Arnold and making sure the trains ran on time. But I wanted to write it all—superheroes, cowboys, vampires, you name it—and dreamed of a future when I'd finally let loose the chained-up stories in my heart.

The intercom buzzed. "Jean," I said, "got yourself pen and paper handy?"

"What do you take me for, an imbecile?"

"Never, Miss Fanning. Never!" I turned my chair toward the great luminosity of grand Manhattan. "I want you to dial up Majesty Modeling. Say you're looking for ad buys in *Love Story* and keep talking till you get to the top of the food chain. Find out whether or not the boss man has kids. If he does, I want you to offer him a year's supply of any book we publish courtesy of yours truly. If he doesn't, offer him a few ads for free. The only thing I'm asking for in return is the phone number of one Valerie St. James."

I could practically hear Jean rolling her eyes. "Really? You're using your power and influence to win a date? How desperate can a man get?"

"What power and influence? Come on, Jean. Do you want me to end up a spinster?"

The intercom clicked off, and although Jean Fanning hadn't answered, I trusted she was at that very moment tracking down the number for Majesty Modeling and getting to work. She liked to tease me, but I never questioned her loyalties. On her first day, she tripped and spilled coffee on a stack of files meant for Benson McCrae. He wanted to fire her on the spot, but I intervened and the rest was history. Jean Fanning was my sister-in-arms.

I spent the start of every morning whispering ideas into my Dictaphone for the comic that would save Zeitgeist, but they were all doughy and unformed like an unfinished baby. I had some snippets of dialogue and a few doodles from Dick Arnold, but that was it. I knew I wanted a superhero family, but beyond that, the details remained fuzzy. I wanted something that symbolically mirrored my journey from Edison to Zeitgeist, how I had abandoned the devastated husk of my family for this new band of merry surrogates, this roving band of creatives who loved and understood me. We had no pasts at Zeitgeist, and I wanted to imbue our comic with a similar sense of freedom and wonder. But the particulars escaped me. Who were these characters? What were their powers? Where did they live?

The intercom interrupted me for the second time that morning, Jean's voice stiff and professional. "Mr. McCrae to see you, Mr. Giordano."

I pressed the button. "Send him in, Jean."

Benson McCrae entered before I could even finish my response, fingering his suspenders, lit stogie stinking up the joint.

"Morning, boss," I tried.

"Don't 'morning' me. I just got my seventh call this month about stacks of Zeitgeist comics sitting untouched and unsold on newsstands. What do you have to say for yourself? What are you doing to save these books?"

"Dick Arnold and I are working on a new project. We just need some time."

"I hired you to maintain a level of quality within all our titles, and that isn't happening."

"Well, maybe I could write some of the titles? We've talked about this before."

The publisher shrugged. "I didn't hire you to write."

"Mr. McCrae, these people out there are doing good work. They're good people. We're giving it all we have."

"I don't care if they're nuns. If they can't sell product, they're of no use to me." McCrae sat and blew a big puff of smoke into my face. "Look. I'm not a bad fella. I'm not Lord Zalbot the Third from *Zap*. Do you know I collect wine? Sure. I have a wine cellar and everything. I'm into classical music. I go to church. I have a full and complete life outside of work that you don't even know about. I'm one of the good guys. But here's the reality. Sales are in the toilet, and Mr. Reeves is close to axing the whole comics division. We're getting the monthly sales report tomorrow. You better pray for a miracle, kid."

I nodded. The alluded-to Mr. Reeves was the ancient owner of Zeitgeist Publishing, a man who wore a kitten-shaped toupee and never left his Central Park high-rise. I'd never met him and knew McCrae would never argue with him on our behalf. McCrae also ran the periodical and book divisions, and whenever he arrived on the seventh floor had the look of a man who just stepped on gum.

And just like that, Benson McCrae was gone. I opened my desk drawer and took a romantic gander at my unopened bottle of I.W. Harper. Dick gifted it to me for Christmas, but I never touched it, didn't believe in getting sloshed on the job. So after an hour of sober flagellation, angelic Jean rang me for the third time on the intercom and delivered the first good news of the day: she'd secured the phone number of the one and only Valerie St. James. I knew this would require all my derring-do, that a woman like Valerie St. James wouldn't be won over by the sad-sack musings of a Madison Avenue pencil pusher.

"Hiya, darling," I said into the phone. "This is Christopher Giordano calling to thank you for a positively delightful evening at old Vincent's."

A long pause. "How did you get this number?"

"A magician never reveals his secrets," I said.

"Golly, you are a piece of work, Giordano. What do you want?"

"Just dinner and drinks on me. You name the time. I've got a standing reservation at the Rainbow Room."

"Are you serious?"

"Sure. Come on. A free dinner won't kill you. Are you really going to say no to a decorated war hero? I earned ten Purple Hearts, baby!"

She sighed. "All right. Tonight at six. No rain checks. You say yes, or I'm hanging up forever."

I rubbed my knees. Six was when I was supposed to meet Dick Arnold to develop our industry-saving superhero book. I thought about how I might explain all this to Valerie when I was suddenly struck by the image of her hands, those delicate tools capable of granting me entry into a world I'd forever been barred from. "Six it is, darling. What's your address?"

I hung up and made a note to tell Jean to reschedule my meeting. I reassured myself that everything was OK, and everything was justified. I was Christopher Giordano from Edison, New Jersey, and the world owed me a night on the town with a British hand model. I would not end up like my father.

• • •

By ten to six, I was zooming through the canyons of Manhattan in a candy apple–red Delahaye 135. The wind ruffled my hair, and oh what a feeling it was to park in front of an elegant apartment building in Chelsea to await the fairest maiden from all of Britain. The sexy coupe wasn't mine, but I knew a car salesman on the Upper West Side hot for *Uncle Cowboy*. Whenever I needed a car, I gifted him a year's subscription free of charge. I'd pulled the same stunt with the maître d' at the Rainbow Room. People all across Manhattan wanted funny books, and sure, maybe they weren't willing to pay for them, but at least I could use what influence I had to borrow their assets and convince sweet Valerie that I, a twenty-three-year-old artiste-on-the-make, was worthy of her attention.

She appeared in a dark green dress cinched at the waist, a matching hat, and dark gloves that concealed those delicious digits. Valerie opened the side door and raised her left eyebrow. "Well, look at the stereotypical American in his big, loud machine."

Before Valerie could even fasten her seatbelt, I stomped the gas and thundered down the street. "Miss St. James, please. This top-of-the-line auto is French."

Located atop the sixty-fifth floor of the RCA Building, the Rainbow Room provided diners with a panoramic view of Manhattan and the finest plate of Lobster Newburg this side of Maryland. I only resorted to the Delahaye and Rainbow Room for peak misadventures, but Valerie St. James remained unimpressed as the maître d' led us to our table, the band belting out ballads. There was something permanently unsurprised about Valerie St. James, and I half-believed that if King Kong scaled the building and scooped her into his furry mitt, Valerie would roll her eyes, perhaps lobbing some sarcastic barb about how she could really go for a brandy.

We ordered drinks and embarked upon a bender the likes of which had surely never been witnessed in the graceful Rainbow Room. The alcohol flowed like water, and, after a plate of Tomato Alexandra, Valerie produced a cigar and puffed it like a plantation owner. The dam broke and one revelation after another came flooding out. We were just kids! Drunken, stupid kids!

"When I was a girl," she told me, "I watched my father kill a doe for sport. It ruined me in some fundamental way."

"I always worry," I said, "that my voice is an octave too high to be successful."

"Sometimes I down three sidecars and go to the cinema alone."

"The only time I ever left the tristate area was when I was stationed in Georgia."

"Once, in Holland, I came across a beggar child who was missing both eyes. He was screaming for bread, and I walked right by him like I hadn't even heard."

"I have this weird lump on the back on my neck. I don't know what it is. I showed it to my secretary."

"I really don't have much interest in men, women, other people in general. I grew up well-off, and I just don't care about anything. It feels like everyone else sees the world in Technicolor, and I'm trapped in black-and-white."

"I'm terrified of dying poor," I said.

Our Lobster Newburgs arrived, and I knew they would be wasted. I would've happily devoured a slow roasted poodle. "Hey," Valerie said, slicing through her biscuit, "you never told me how you got into funny books. How'd that happen?"

Valerie St. James removed her gloves, and there was something about this act—the long-awaited debut of those glorious appendages—that dislodged something hard behind my chest, some final barrier between me and the truth.

"Funny story," I said. "My baby sister Angela got me into them. She always had these stacks of *Action Comics, Detective Comics,* the works. You know them? Superman and Batman?"

Valerie nodded through a bite of lobster. "Yes. We have them in England."

"I loved the idea—Superman, a man who couldn't die. You know I met the boys who created him. They dreamed him up after one of their dads was killed in a robbery."

"You don't say," Valerie said, voice distant.

"My sister was always sick. Got tuberculosis. Couldn't do much but read." I looked at my hands. "She died six years ago."

This piqued her interest. "That must have been hard on you."

"Sure."

"Hard on your family."

"I was seventeen. I was drafted not long after. I never go back."

"You never see your parents?" Valerie asked.

"My mom died when I was a kid. My dad? It's difficult." I moved the ruined architecture of my biscuit. "He doesn't understand this." I gestured around the Rainbow Room. "He doesn't see why anyone would want to leave New Jersey where everything smells like tomatoes and garlic."

We were quiet then. The band broke into a song I didn't recognize, and this mystery felt appropriate. I had come to the Rainbow Room to wow Valerie St. James, and instead I'd managed to drunkenly summon the ghost of my sister while revealing my poor performance as a son.

"You know," Valerie said, pointing at me, "you remind me of someone, and I finally put my finger on it."

"Who's that?"

"My kid brother."

• • •

I was thirty minutes late to work the next morning. Not because of anything Valerie-related—I dropped her off within an hour of the "kid brother" bomb—but because I woke up mildly hungover. Nothing too heavy, nothing like the benders we eager soldiers of Fort Benning embarked upon during leave. I realized my error the moment I entered Zeitgeist and saw the frazzled look across Jean Fanning's face.

"Your phone's been ringing off the hook, Christopher," she said. "First it was your father. Then it was Dick Arnold. He's mad you canceled on him yesterday, and he's coming in to finalize your new project. He's got designs. But then it was McCrae. He's been calling once every seven minutes since we opened. I timed it."

"Why didn't he just come down?"

"He didn't say. You should call your father back."

"Next time McCrae calls, you put him right through."

My office was the same as ever, but it felt unfamiliar. Something about revealing the trauma of my youth to another person made me feel as if I'd resurrected my teenage self, like he and Angela were tailing me all over Manhattan. I wondered how my view of the city would look to them or my father. I'd gone to the tanning factory a few times as a boy and even then was aware of its lack of windows and odor of burning rubber and boiled eggs. I felt like an imposter in my suit, an imposter with fake war stories and a borrowed coupe and the Rainbow Room. The intercom buzzed with Jean's familiar voice. "McCrae's on the line."

The call was fuzzy, and I knew immediately my boss was far from Manhattan.

"Where the hell have you been?" he demanded.

"My train was late."

"That book you're dreaming up with Arnold? Is it finished?"

I rubbed at my temple. "Not exactly."

"Figures. So here's the deal, kid. I've got amazing news. I've thought long and hard about your aspirations as a writer. We all think you have a bright future with us at Zeitgeist, so we're giving you a crack at scripting duties. *Zap, Tomb of the Living Vampire, Uncle Cowboy, Love Story, Baby Stevie,* and *The New Adventures of Warlock*. Congratulations, kid."

I stared at the intercom. Nobody in the decade-long history of Zeitgeist Comics had ever been entrusted to write six monthly books. I didn't even know if that was possible, especially if I was still expected to perform my editorial duties. In even my grandest fantasies I assumed McCrae would start me on a single low-selling book.

"What do you say, Giordano?"

"I'm stunned, sir. Thrilled."

"Good, because the monthly sales report came in late last night, and it was horseshit. We're talking thousands of unsold comics, and the newsstands are demanding refunds. Reeves is going nuts. He's ordered me to cancel the worst selling nineteen books, ax the staff save for one assistant editor, and hire some art students to draw interiors/exteriors. Congrats, Giordano. You're the sole survivor of Zeitgeist Comics."

"You're joking," I blurted.

"You know I don't joke, Giordano. The layoffs take effect starting immediately. It's hard news, but that's the industry. A few of them will find work at DC or Atlas. We're not the only game in town."

"Can I just have a few more days to hammer out my book with Arnold? Mr. McCrae, I'm telling you, it can turn things around."

"You're too late, Christopher. Maybe down the line, but now's not the time."

"Why aren't you telling me this in person?"

A window washer across the street scaled up the exterior of his building in a wooden pulley. "That's the other thing," McCrae said. "After Reeves told me, I booked a flight to Hawaii. A long overdue vacation. I'm no good at firing folks, so that's on you, kid. It should only take you the rest of the day."

"And if I refuse?"

"Then we fire you too."

And so: I could be sacrificed with the rest of the Merry Bullpen of Zeitgeist Comics or take my dream job and announce to Manhattan and the wider world beyond that I was a person of worth, filled to bursting with bright and fantastic stories. It wasn't that fantasy that made me decide, but a memory of my father coming home from work, how he'd stand in the doorway and shed his work boots, grease-stained gloves, the creased denim that had turned soft in the years of service rendered to the tanning factory.

"All right," I told McCrae. "All right."

"Fantastic, Giordano. I knew we chose the right man for the job. I just knew it. Now remember, you're the boss now. You look those bastards right in the eye, and you slice at the neck. No remorse. No mercy. Do it like Normandy. For the Allies, am I right?"

• • •

In the beginning, it wasn't so bad. Jean Fanning called Bill Polymer—a cover artist we'd grifted from Timely two weeks earlier—and I calmly explained that the powers-that-be had eliminated his position. Sure, Bill was peeved and swiped three pencils from my desk before leaving, but his anger didn't sweep through the office. Not yet anyway. "Jean," I said into the intercom, "send Mary Walsh next."

By the end of the hour, I'd fired Polymer, Walsh, Fritz, Lewis, and "Peaches" Salvatore. I still remember each and every one of their names, and I still remember their individual reactions—the way Fritz crumpled his hands, how "Peaches" Salvatore produced a tin of peaches and devoured them right on the spot, how a single tear rolled down Fritz's cheek. After the sixth firing, the Bullpen knew something was up, and I saw them lining up outside my office, demanding to know what in Sam Hill was going on. Freddie Lancaster shouted that he wasn't going to putz around all day just to be fired by "that flute playing Nancy boy five minutes to five." "Send Freddie in next," I told Jean.

Then Johnson, Smertz, Darlish, Diaz, Fontaine. Then Gerber, Kirby, Fauxburger, Claremont, and Simon. Then Chalmers, Orrington, Fontana, Segel, and McVey.

That made twenty-six, and it felt like as good a place as any to take a break. It was lunch time, and my hands were shaking—badly ever since McVey hurled his cufflinks at me—and I reached into my drawer for Dick Arnold's I.W. Harper and poured a mighty drink fit for Dionysius. These were the people who had taken me in after my admittedly pathetic "service" during World War II. These were the men and women who had accepted me with open arms after I traded Edison for the big apple of New York. Jean's voice was steady on the intercom as I demanded the presence of one employee after another. In retrospect, I should have cut Jean loose first, but the truth was I couldn't imagine enduring that ghoulish task, without hearing her sing-song voice every few minutes.

McGuire, Clocks, Morning, McEnroe, and Raymond "The Hammer" Worthington fell next. "The Hammer" simply walked into my office, called me a drunk, and walked out. They could smell on it me by then. The room wasn't quite spinning when "The Hammer" left, but I knew that before the day ended, I'd find myself spewing my internals all over the porcelain toilet in my Hoboken abode.

Finally, I reached the end. It was almost five, I was sloshed, and I'd offed thirty-nine Zeitgeist employees in a row, everybody but me, Jean, and Dick Arnold. I opened my door, and for the first time I heard nothing. No chatter. No clanking on typewriters. No furious erasing. The Merry Bullpen had been silenced, and I saw Jean Fanning glaring at me.

"Christopher?" she asked.

"Is Dick Arnold on his way?"

"He should be here any minute."

I returned to my desk and offered her a glass. "You want some bourbon, sweetheart? It's the good stuff."

Jean said nothing, and it was only then when I realized she was wearing her coat and gloves.

"Why are you dressed to leave, Jean?"

"I've been dressed like this since you fired Linda."

I nodded and leaned back in my chair. I'd finished my fourth glass of Harper and thought, hey, to hell with pretenses and took a swig straight from the bottle. "Jean." I liked repeating her name and wished I'd said it more when I had the chance. "Did I ever tell you that you remind me of my sister, Angela? She died of TB when we were just kids."

"Mr. Giordano. I don't give a flying hoot about your sister. That death doesn't make you unique. My fiancé died in Wallonia, Belgium, during the war. Everyone our age is more than familiar with death. If you think for a second that your loss somehow makes up for the way you've behaved today, you're wrong." It was obvious to me even in my sorry state that she'd been rehearsing this speech all day. "Don't think for a second that anything you say now will excuse what you've done. You fired an entire office, Christopher. An entire office! This is a tiny industry. People will always remember you for this. You've behaved like a monster."

Another swig. "What should I have done? You tell me. Really. What was I supposed to do?"

"Go down with the ship. Refuse to be McCrae's hatchet man. You could've gotten another position at Timely or DC or Archie. But not now. People will remember this," she repeated.

I dropped my head to my hands. "I couldn't risk it."

"Risk what?"

I knew the answer hummed inside me somewhere, but I didn't have the lexicon to articulate it, not to Jean or myself. And when it was clear I had nothing left to say, Jean opened my office door and left. Waiting was none other than Dick Arnold, a stern look on his face. He put his arms around Jean to comfort her and threw his designs on my floor.

"You're not talented," he said, "and you've disappointed everybody who used to care about you."

They both left, and I was at last alone. I sat there for another four hours watching the sun fall behind Hoboken, casting Zeitgeist into darkness.

• • •

By ten, I'd killed the bottle of Harper. By midnight, I'd finished off two more lonely drinks in Vincent's, empty that time on a Thursday. By one, I stepped off the train and zigzagged to the tenement I shared with fourteen other desperate souls on the west end of Hoboken. I never, ever, for any reason, brought anyone where I lived. It was a cramped little building wedged on a narrow street that smelled perpetually of liver and onions. I tiptoed up the stairs—careful not to disturb Mrs. Washington, the landlord who oversaw our lives like a nun—and slipped into my apartment, a studio with a bed next to the toilet. I ran my head under the faucet before deciding that I wasn't done yet, that this bender had not truly run its course. I retrieved another bottle of bourbon from the closet—the cheap stuff—and took a few swigs. Then I slumped to the phone in the hallway and dialed her number.

Valerie St. James answered, and even dead asleep she didn't sound groggy or unrefined. Only twenty-four hours had passed since our evening at the Rainbow Room, but it felt like weeks, months, years.

"Christopher? Why are you calling at this hour?"

"Look, I'm sorry but I have to know. Why do some people grow up like you and some people grow up like me?"

"What are you talking about?"

"I need someone to explain it to me. Please. Just tell me what the—"

She hung up, and I did not see her again until thirty years later when I was a slightly happier person. It was at a party thrown by Jackie Donato in the Hollywood Hills when I was in talks with some studios about bringing my superheroes to the silver screen—they never went anywhere. My wife and I were having a gay old time when I saw Valerie St. James standing quietly at the poolside bar. We'd both aged in the interim, but I recognized her immediately on account of those hands which were still immaculate, which even then represented some status or class I knew I could never access. Nothing would ever fill the gaping maw I cultivated back in Edison. I saw Valerie from across the pool, our faces glowing, and we locked eyes. We didn't speak. But in that moment, she recognized me and gave a little wave. It seemed so much more important than it was, and I felt so taken aback that I retreated inside the house, my wife asking, "What's wrong? Christopher, what's wrong?" All I could picture was Jean Fanning's face.

But that future was very much ahead of me as I stood slumped in the hallways of my Hoboken tenement. I took a few more sips of bourbon and dialed one final number, my father's, forever burned into my brain. To this day, so many decades removed from his death, I can still recite it like a lullaby.

"Hullo?"

It was so peculiar to hear his voice again. This was the man who had raised me, and yet I'd barely spoken to him since leaving home. I wondered if he looked how I remembered, and if when he pictured me now, he saw me as I was or the way I appeared as a child, when his family was still fully alive.

"Dad," I slurred. "It's me. I just want to . . . I'm sorry I left you, Dad. I'm so sorry I left you. I'm so sorry I left you. I'm so fucking sorry for everything I've done."

The Absolutely True Autobiography of Tony Rinaldi, the Man Who Changed Pro Wrestling Forever

Chapter 6: 1982

The morning after my father's funeral, I called Billy Chen into the office and told him to get Winston Hamilton on the line. Chen was my father's best friend and right-hand man for twenty-five years, and he just stared at me with this hangdog expression like he couldn't believe I was asking him to work less than twenty-four hours after burying the old man.

"He was *my* father, goddamn it. Now get me Hamilton." I pressed the phone to my ear and waited. "Winston," I said, "how's Minneapolis, pal? This is Tony Rinaldi from the World Wrestling Alliance."

"Tony?" He paused. "I'm sorry about your daddy. He loved the business more than anybody."

"Yeah. Thanks, pal." I kicked my feet up over the desk. "But I'm actually calling about you. So your father went ahead and made you champ, huh? Congratulations! Long overdue. How's the run going? Word in New York is attendance's in the shitter."

Another long pause. We both knew he was under contract with the AWA for another four years. "What's this about, Tony?"

"I want a meeting with you, your wife, and Metalhead. Tonight."

"Where? Here?"

Chen waved his arms and shook his head no, no, no.

"Absolutely, pal," I said. "The jet's gassed up, and we already made reservations tonight at . . . Murray's, right? Ric Flair's favorite steakhouse?"

"Tony, you ribbing me?"

"Absolutely not, pal. I got Billy 'The Loudmouth' Chen with me right now dying to see you. Figured this would be a great time to touch base and finally meet the Mrs. I hear Maria has an aptitude for the business. That right, Winston? But your father's not keen on using her as a manager?"

One of my cardinal rules of negotiation is to always highlight the personal. Anyone who claims business is only business is either stupid or a liar. We're dumb sacks of meat who make decisions based on personal bullshit 100 times out of 100.

"OK," Winston finally said. "We'll see you at Murray's tonight."

I hung up and grinned at Chen, the best damn manager I'd ever seen. Pass him a mic and march him to the center of the ring in Madison Square Garden and that bastard lit up the place, spit flying like a Southern preacher. But in his private life, Billy "The Loudmouth" Chen was quiet and thoughtful to a fault. He sighed and said, "I'll arrange the jet and make the dinner reservations."

"Goddamn right you will, pal. Goddamn right."

• • •

So right about now is when my third biographer is essentially forcing me at gunpoint to tell you a little bit more about my relationship with my father and the whole state of the business by '82. Why I have to listen to some pencil-neck writer from Binghamton is beyond me, but listen up, Gordie Mancini, I can fire your ass just like I fired the others, so don't you dare edit this goddamn gold out.[1]

---

1. Mr. Rinaldi threatened to breach contract if we didn't include this rant. —GM

Reader, you may have noticed that perhaps I breezed over my childhood at the start of this very fine biography that only cost you a cool $7.99. In the pro wrestling business, we have a saying: the only thing that matters is what you're about to do. OK. I just made that up, but it's true. Nobody cares about how well you drew[2] in Albuquerque three years ago. Can you pack them to the rafters in Utica tonight? If not, crawl the fuck home to your wife and kids, pal. Why should I begin my biography with my childhood when my real life, what I consider to be my true life, started when I entered the wrestling business at the tender age of eighteen? But fine. I'll give in to goddamn Gordie Mancini this one time. I mean, the man's published a coming-of-age sci-fi novel! What a prestigious writer! He must know what he's doing, right, folks?

I was born in Scranton, Pennsylvania, on August 24, 1945, three months after the Allies declared victory over World War II. My mother, this frail, quiet bird, told me my daddy died gunning down Nazis, and the two of us lived in the bad part of town called the Plot. It flooded every year and everybody's basement reeked of mold. She remarried when I was seven. A drunken Irish miner who beat the shit out of us every time the Steelers lost even though Pittsburgh was five hours west on I-80. I crippled him with a crowbar when I was seventeen, and the next year I won a football scholarship to Rutgers. The night before I skipped town for good, my mother told me the truth about my father.[3]

She drove me to the Glider Diner, just me and her, and you people

---

2. This is an old carnival term for earning money. If a show sold out, credit usually went to the wrestlers in the main event, i.e., Winston Hamilton really drew the sellout in Minneapolis. —GM

3. Very little of this can be verified. Goliath Publishing has been unable to produce a birth certificate for anyone named Tony Rinaldi born in Scranton, Pennsylvania, in 1945, and we assume this is a stage name meant to match his father's and that much of Mr. Rinaldi's biography presented here is either embellished or completely falsified. What we know for sure is he grew up in the northeastern coal region of Pennsylvania in the late-forties and fifties under a woman of very modest means and that he didn't meet his father until he was eighteen, after he won a football scholarship to Rutgers. Whether or not Mr. Rinaldi knew his father's identity growing up is questionable, but, based on his father's unpublished autobiography, Michael Rinaldi knew he had a son and never tried to contact him. —GM

have to understand this was big time for little old Tony Rinaldi and his dear old ma. We didn't go out to eat very often, and never without that crippled Irishman. "Tony," Mama said, big fat tears rimming her eyes, "goddamn it, there's something I never told you."

"What the fuck is it, Ma?"

She didn't even own a hanky, so she had to blow her nose in a diner napkin like a goddamn peasant. "Your daddy didn't die gunning down Nazis in the great Second World War!"

"Ma!" I shouted. "How can this be?"

"His name is Michael Rinaldi. You used to watch him on the teevee set. He runs the World Wrestling Alliance out in evil New York City."

Well, readers, I'll be honest with you. I didn't think too much of Michael Rinaldi right then. No, sir. A daddy who died sniping fascists in the Hürtgen Forest? That's something to puff your chest out over. A man who ignored me my whole life and ran a fake fighting ring for drunken immigrants fresh off the boat in Manhattan? No thank you. I'd watched his program growing up. Had seen and maybe even enjoyed wrestlers like Iron Thompson and the Garbanzos and, yes, even Billy "The Loudmouth" Chen before he blew out his damn knee caps and pivoted to manager full-time. But there was no time for fake fighting when you had a drunken Irish coal miner rampaging through the trailer like a goddamn bull!

So, off I go to Rutgers, and everything is fantastic, pal, just fantastic, but I have to admit my natural curiosity got the better of me. It's one of my greatest assets, pal. Don't edit this out, Gordie. Rutgers is less than an hour from New York, so I rode the train to the Garden and watched NWA champion Larry "The Bruiser" Pilsner square off with WWA champ Veteran Vinnie Valentine. In those days, the entire American wrestling business was broken up into twelve territories under the National Wrestling Alliance banner. The owners of all the territories voted on the next NWA champion, and then the champ would travel from promotion to promotion getting the local talent over.[4] Everybody collectively profited, and nobody ever went

4. An old carnival term for making a wrestler popular with the crowd. —GM

rogue or stole talent from another promotion or invaded another territory. My father and his generation lived by a code of honor, just like the Mafia. I didn't know any of that then though. I was just a pimply kid from Scranton gawking in the rafters with my Cracker Jacks.

I watched Pilsner and Valentine fight sixty goddamn minutes to a no-contest, and the crowd just ate it up, hooting and hollering, cursing Pilsner when he showboated, pleading with Vinnie not to submit to the dreaded Carolina Chokehold. There's a lot of talk these days about how I outed the business for what it is: a work, not a shoot.[5] But the truth is: everybody other than the kids knew something was fishy. How could you not with the flashy entrances and the drama of it all and the way the boys would go ten, twenty seconds without even trying to attack each other? Sure, maybe some inbreds down in West Virginia thought it was real, but in Madison Square Garden, everybody was in on the gag, and they all played their roles—the wrestlers, refs, ring announcers, even the thousands of us in the crowd. There's something magic about that. And there's something god-damn stupid about that. It really intrigued me.

After the show, I snuck backstage and told my father who I was. "Tony," he said, "goddamn it, I wish you respected me enough the way I respect you to never, ever contact me. But since you're here, grab a fucking broom, pal." He offered me a part-time gig selling autographed glossies of the wrestlers, and I worked my way up the ladder for twenty years all the way to VP. On his deathbed, he made everyone leave the room but me and offered to sell me the WWA for half-a-million dollars.[6] He needed the cash for his legitimate kids. They played violin or something and wanted nothing to do

---

5. More old carnival terms. A work means faked, while a shoot is legitimate. For example, a boxing match is a shoot, while pro wrestling is a work. —GM

6. What Mr. Rinaldi has refused to explain in his writing is that his wife, a rich debutante from Connecticut and daughter of a railroad tycoon, helped fund his purchase of the WWA. Mr. Rinaldi met his wife at Rutgers shortly after seeing his father for the first time in New York, and, since 1983, she's served as the VP of the World Wrestling Alliance. Unfortunately, due to her high-level appointment in the Trump administration, Mr. Rinaldi insists that we not use her name in the book or ever reference her more than this single time. I, Gordie Mancini, would like it known that I fought this editorial decision tooth and nail. —GM

with the business. "Tony," he said, "be grateful I'm even allowing you the opportunity to buy the business. Never forget you're the bastard." Then he croaked from lung cancer. He never told me he loved me if that's what you jackals are after. Is that enough, Gordie Mancini? Does that explain my relationship to my father now?[7]

• • •

I snuck the private jet through during my father's cancer. He never appreciated glitz and glamour and believed pro wrestling was low-class entertainment and only our heels[8] should appear rich or high-falutin'. But I saw the writing on the walls and wanted to push pro wrestling into the neon lights of the 1980s. My father never got it, and neither did Loudmouth, not at first. He sulked on that jet en route to Minneapolis with the glummest expression I'd ever seen. You would have thought his father up and croaked, goddamn it.[9]

---

7. Firsthand accounts of Tony Rinaldi's relationship with his father are difficult to ascertain. Michael Rinaldi's best friend and Tony Rinaldi's right-hand man, Billy "The Loudmouth" Chen, told Dingo Blue in a 2013 YouTube shoot interview that "they were always cold with each other. Never had a warm relationship. Michael treated me like his son even though we were the same age, and Tony treated me like his father. He didn't even go to the funeral. Went to Buzzer's in Long Island and drank half the bar." But, in Sheriff Justice's autobiography, ***Justice Comes to Town***, Justice wrote, "And this goes without saying, my friends, but nobody in this business was more broken up about Mikey Rinaldi's passing than his son. They'd spent two decades working side-by-side. That changes a man. At the funeral, I saw Tony hidden in the shadows bawling his eyes out like a kid. It was the only time I ever saw him vulnerable." —GM

8. An old carnival term for villain. A hero is a babyface, baby, or face. —GM

9. Rumors and innuendo abound that Billy "The Loudmouth" Chen and Michael Rinaldi engaged in a long-term romantic relationship that was a somewhat open secret among the wrestlers backstage. Although no concrete evidence exists minus shoot interviews and biographies from second-hand sources, Michael Rinaldi left the deed to a small beachside property in Martha's Vineyard to Chen in his will. In private letters to the Soul Brother obtained after his death, Rinaldi wrote that his house on the Vineyard was "the only place in the world where I feel like I'm not playing a character." Chen never wrote a will, so, after his death from liver failure in 2016, the deed turned over to the banks. —GM

Finally, I couldn't take it anymore. I took a leak, then came back and snuck up behind Loudmouth all quiet and fucking grabbed him in a choke-hold. I handled the business sides of things and announced matches for our TV show on Saturdays,[10] but I loved working out with the boys and had the pythons to prove it. We all horsed around backstage, but this time Loudmouth was pissed. He could turn truly angry. I'd seen it. When fans shouted racial slurs at him, he would leap into the crowd and throw a jab that would knock down a drunk before you could even blink. In the jet, Loudmouth tossed me into the aisle and potatoed[11] me three times in the gut. I got my licks in though. Don't you worry about old Tony Rinaldi, goddamn it. But the stewardess? She just stood there holding our glasses of merlot with this shocked look on her face. I think she's the only reason we stopped.

"What's your fucking problem, Loudmouth?" I asked when I returned to my seat.

He looked out the window. "You know exactly what my problem is."

"What? A guy can't treat his buddy to a quick trip to Minneapolis? Don't we deserve it? We work hard."

He snatched both glasses from the stewardess and gulped them down like water. "This isn't the way we do business, Tony."

---

10. The original World Wrestling Alliance television program, ***Saturday Superstars***, is one of the first examples of how radically Tony Rinaldi's vision of pro wrestling differed from his father's and the rest of the NWA's. Most wrestling programs of the 1970s were low-budget affairs focused on gritty workers, long in-ring matches, and the occasional short interview. Often, they resembled public access programs more than anything on the major networks. But when Tony Rinaldi took over ***Saturday Superstars*** in 1980 after his father's health began to decline, he immediately upped the production values with flashy lights and rock music. The gritty workers were replaced by cartoony characters like Sheriff Justice, Uncle Sam, and the Taxman, and few matches lasted longer than five or six minutes, that time now dedicated to interviews with wrestlers and the occasional musician or actor who appealed to kids and teenagers. Between 1972 and 1981, ***Saturday Superstars*** only aired in the Northeast, but after Michael Rinaldi's death in 1982, Tony Rinaldi immediately pushed for syndication and national expansion. To directly compete with other territories' wrestling shows, he needed talent their fans already knew. Hence, his quest for Winston Hamilton and other main eventers like him. —GM

11. An old carnival term for a shoot punch instead of a worked punch. —GM

"No," I said. "This isn't the way my father did business. This is the way we're doing business moving forward, pal."

"Your father believes . . . believed in the territory system. No poaching. No invading. When a talent turns stale, send him to a new territory where he's fresh. Everyone profits." Loudmouth finally met my eyes. "They're going to kick you out of the NWA if you steal Minnesota's champion mid-contract. Come on, Tony. Winston Hamilton works for his dad."[12]

I stared at my loafers, the very same I'd worn to my father's funeral. We didn't speak for the rest of the flight.

• • •

Everybody knew about Murray's in Minneapolis on account of Ric Flair. He grew up in the 'burbs and basically banged and boozed the entire state dry before his seventeenth birthday. It was an old-style chop house with class—white linens, candles, shrimp cocktails—the kind of pizzazz that impressed wrestlers who spent most of their lives on the road, driving from one shit town to the next living out of Ramada Inns off the highway and inhaling McDonald's. Loudmouth and I arrived thirty minutes early, another one of my business philosophies. Always be early to a meeting, then spread out, make the space yours. You want whoever you're meeting to feel like they're entering your home. Then, you already have an advantage even if Winston lived ten minutes away, and we'd flown in from New York.

You couldn't miss them when they walked through the door. Winston Hamilton was a goddamn physical specimen if I ever saw one. Looked like a bodybuilder with this cocky smile and long golden locks like some kind of Nordic jester. Plus, the boy could work. His moves looked stiff,[13] and even though he played babyface in Minneapolis, there was potential for a heel

---

12. Knuckles Hamilton was a legendary Minnesotan wrestler who purchased the AWA territory after his retirement in 1977. As owner, Knuckles immediately pushed his son, Winston, as the heir apparent to the Minnesota territory. —GM

13. An old carnival term that means the wrestler's moves looked real, more like a shoot than a work. —GM

run down the road. His wife and Metalhead were only passable though. I'd studied the tapes for weeks. Maria was a knockout, but couldn't do shit on the mic, was totally tongue-tied. Plus, the reason Knuckles Hamilton and the AWA never used her as Winston's manager is the moment you pair a pretty lady with a babyface, the fans boo the babyface. A pretty lady on your arm doesn't make people root for you. They envy and despise you. That's what Ric Flair always understood. And Metalhead? Totally generic heel. Real name was Sanchez. Couldn't sell for shit, and all he could do in the ring were these power slams and clotheslines. His ceiling was jobbing to midcard faces and prepping them for top heels, and I had plenty of those bad boys back in New York. No, Winston Hamilton was the prize, the twenty-four-year-old champion of the AWA, son of the legendary Knuckles Hamilton, a wrestler known across the country. But if I wanted Winston to turn his back on the AWA and his father and the entire territorial system, I needed to provide a few extra incentives. That meant his ambitious wife and underutilized best friend.

I stood and held out my arms. "Hamilton! Mrs. Hamilton! Sanchez! So happy you could join us. We come here all the time. We just love Murray's, right, Loudmouth?"

Loudmouth blinked at the floor. "Yes."

I made a big show of ordering three bottles of wine and a bunch of shrimp cocktails. Another business tip: get 'em wasted, and never talk business before everybody's done with the main course. We listened to Sinatra and Dean and the lesser members of the Rat Pack, and me and Loudmouth just smiled and nodded as Maria explained the pros and cons of Minneapolis and her father-in-law's AWA. Hamilton met her during a loop from Austin down into Mexico City, and it was obvious after two minutes that she was both the brains and heart of their chummy little trio.

"Oh, Mr. Rinaldi," she said, glass half-full, "we've seen your Saturday show. It's big, flashy, very hip, but it would never work up here. You know this is AWA country through and through. It's old-school storytelling."

I smiled wide. "Maybe we can change that."

Hamilton chewed his last slice of bloody steak. "I'm real sorry about your pops, Tony. Everyone in the business respected him. He's a legend in the NWA."

I nodded and held up my glass. I understood how much the boys looked up to my father, how they'd probably known his name since they were tykes. "A toast to my old man." We drank, and no one, and I mean no one, sipped longer than one Tony Rinaldi. "But let's forget about the past for a minute, OK? Let's talk future."

Sanchez balled up his napkin and tossed it on his plate. "There's not much to say, Tony. I'm sorry you flew all the way out here, but Winston's under contract for the next four years, and I'm locked up for three. Maybe we could talk about the WWA then, but our hands are tied."

I looked Sanchez in the eyes. "You were a masked luchador down in Tijuana, right?"

He fidgeted with his fork. "My father was buried in his mask. Yeah, you could say I was a masked luchador all right."

"Me and Loudmouth have seen the tapes, haven't we, Loudmouth?"

Loudmouth hadn't spoken to anyone other than the waiter. "Yes," he managed.

"El Martillo," I said. "Great gimmick. Could really get over in the States. We have a large Mexican population in New York. We could bring you in as El Martillo the heel, then turn you baby. Could draw huge."

Sanchez's face was unchanged.

"Knuckles doesn't see a luchador getting over in Minnesota, that right?" I asked.

"That's right," he said.

I turned to Maria and Winston. "Let's cut to brass fucking tacks, kiddos. The WWA's on the verge of exploding. We got Uncle Sam slated for a program with Benji the Giant that's going to culminate in national pay-per-view.[14]

14. No one could have predicted in 1982 that soon Uncle Sam would become one of the most famous athletes in the world, his name synonymous with pro wrestling for the next four decades. Although technically limited in the ring, Uncle Sam was incredibly charismatic, and

That's right. Not some bullshit closed circuit like Crockett[15] uses down south. We're going big time. I'm working a deal to get *Saturday Superstars* in eighteen states by the end of the year. Twenty-eight in '83."

"That's outright invasion into the other territories," Winston said.

"You're goddamn right, pal. This is a war, and I'm going to win it. Men like our fathers? They're carnies. I'm MTV. I have the vision and resources to take this business further than it's ever been. Winston, you're the youngest champion AWA's seen in two decades. How much did you earn last year?"

He was quiet, but then he flinched and coughed up the truth. Maria probably hit him under the goddamn table! Now that's a broad I understood.[16] "Seventy thousand," he said.

"Seventy? That's a crime. You're the champ, goddamn it. I've got enhancement talent[17] making almost that. And what about you, Sanchez? You've been feuding with Winston here in the main event for the better part of six months. What's Knuckles paying you?"

"Fifty," he admitted quietly.

I scribbled figures on a napkin, but I'd already researched their pay months ago, after my father was first diagnosed. "And you, darling Maria? A bombshell with a fantastic head on her shoulders who's ready-made for TV? What's dear old daddy paying you?"

---

his catchphrase, "Americana's running wild, brother!" helped sell over three million Americana Easy Rip T-shirts between 1985 and 1993 before his shocking defection to WCW. —GM

15. An extremely influential wrestling promoter in South Carolina whose territory eventually morphed into WCW—World Championship Wrestling—the WWA's greatest rival. —GM

16. Rumors and innuendo abound that Tony Rinaldi and Maria Hamilton engaged in a long-term romantic relationship. Although no concrete evidence exists minus shoot interviews and biographies from secondhand sources, the affair seemed to be a somewhat open secret among the wrestlers backstage. Whether or not Winston Hamilton ever discovered this affair is equally unknown, but the maid who found him dead from a cocaine overdose in a Chattanooga Motel 6 retrieved a small notepad that may or may not have been a suicide note. The only words scribbled in the pad read, "Rinaldi killed Camelot." Winston Hamilton was thirty-five. —GM

17. An old carnival term for wrestlers whose sole job is to lose and make the bigger stars look strong. —GM

She didn't look away. "Nada."

"Nada!" I turned to Loudmouth. "Can you believe this?"

"No," he said flatly.

"Goddamn right, pal." I straightened my lapels. It's always a good look before going in for the kill. Enhances my pecs and makes me look strong. "Here's the offer. I cover the early termination fees in both your contracts. Then I double both your salaries. Maria, we'll start you at seventy-five. In two weeks' time, Uncle Sam is fighting Crocodile Augustus up in Boston. At the end of the match, Croc pulls out brass knuckles and bloodies up Sam, makes a crimson mess of him in the ring. Then, out of nowhere, AWA's fighting babyface champion Winston Hamilton runs out from the back, and all the while I'm going nuts on commentary." I cupped my hands around my mouth. "This has never happened before in the history of pro wrestling! A champion from another federation running out to save the WWA's biggest star! The crowd will immediately love you for saving Uncle Sam, and then next week we introduce Maria as your valet. We launch you into a program with Croc, and you go over twice on TV. Then, Sanchez shows up as El Martillo and sucker punches sweet Maria from behind. Winston cuts a promo the following week claiming that the AWA title doesn't mean anything to him anymore. You toss it in the trash and vow to avenge Maria, and then we launch into a three-month barn burner between you and Sanchez, culminating in Maria's triumphant return! All three of you become massive stars. Action figures. Video games. Maybe even movies. Rich and goddamn famous."[18]

Maria's eyes were so big that I knew if Winston even suggested turning

---

18. Juan "El Martillo" Sanchez only lasted with the WWA for two years. After that, he floundered in what remained of the NWA before ending his career in the hardcore-centric ECW—Extreme Championship Wrestling. In 1995, Doomsday botched a running powerbomb and dropped Sanchez on his head in Trenton, New Jersey. He was paralyzed from the neck down and has since retired outside Tijuana. Maria Hamilton briefly left pro wrestling in 1993 after the death of her husband, but writer Vince Russo brought her back to the business in 1999 to WCW and again to TNA—Total Nonstop Action—in 2003 before she retired to Mexico City. She was arrested in 2008 on two counts of drug possession and later died of a heart attack in Reno, Nevada. She was forty-nine. —GM

me down, she'd file for divorce within fifteen minutes. But the men looked uneasy. Winston, Sanchez, and especially Loudmouth. Chen had always been loyal to my father, but I knew he'd be even more loyal to me. He might complain, but secretly, deep down, he wanted to learn how big the business could get.

"If the AWA champion jumps ship to your national show," Winston said, "and tosses the fucking belt in the garbage, the AWA will lose all credibility."

"That's the idea."

"You're asking me to screw over my old man."

I shrugged. "Knuckles screwed you over by paying you less than what you deserve and by having an extremely limited vision of what the business is truly capable of."

"The NWA will ban you for this," Sanchez tried.

"Fuck the NWA. You think that council of geezers would give either of you a run at the top? Absolutely not. They still think it's nineteen fucking fifty-five. They make all of us look like morons when they keep pushing forty-year-olds over twenty-somethings. It's absurd." I refilled my wine and tried to calm myself. "I'm going to destroy the NWA and anyone else who gets in my way along with it. The WWA's going national, kids. Coast-to-coast. Let me pay you a compliment, all right? I'm lining up meetings with all the top young stars from every promotion across the country all week long. I reached out to you first. By summer, the NWA will be crippled. If you don't take this offer, you're committing career suicide. I'm offering you a lifeboat off the *Titanic*."

Winston's eyes were pleading and confused, but I knew I had him by the balls. "Tony, why are you doing this?"

I didn't hesitate. "Because my father believed in a code of honor, and I'm going to show everyone how stupid that son of a bitch really was." I turned to Loudmouth. "Pass 'em their contracts, Billy."

They pretended to hem and haw, but we knew it was just for show. Wrestlers are cockroaches—they survive. They escape dead territories and find their way to the boomtowns, then repeat the process over and over again until they finally drop dead, their bodies used up and worthless. They signed. Of course they did. I shook their hands and looked all three of them in the eyes, and the crazy fucking thing, the thing that still gets me is I didn't even see much potential in them. Winston was a good hand, but his ceiling was a midcard baby at best, maybe a tag champ after his solo run fizzled out. El Martillo was too big and low-to-the-ground to get over as a Mexican babyface, and Knuckles was right about Maria. The moment the crowd saw her with Winston, they'd hate him. But I wasn't spending big to acquire them. Not really. I was spending to strike a death blow to the AWA, and then I'd do the same to every NWA promotion in the country. I would borrow myself into oblivion to buy out the competition, then feast off the profits once the WWA cornered the market. We waved goodbye outside, and I wished so badly that my father could see this and everything I was capable of.

We didn't stay overnight in Minneapolis. I needed to run the whole program back the next day in Florida, and I explained this to Loudmouth on the jet before listing my top targets across the territories. The stewardess topped us off with champagne, and Loudmouth was the portrait of a loyal soldier. He took notes, arranged contracts, provided counsel. But an hour or so into our flight, after all my plans for domination were laid bare, he turned to me and said something that's stuck with me over the years.

"Tony," Loudmouth said, "before you do anything else, I just want you to understand how disappointed your father would be. He didn't raise you to be this kind of man."

I put my arm around Chen. He was the same age as my father, and they'd been as intimate as two pals could be. If I have my way, I'll engrave what I told him on my headstone when I croak. "Two things, Loudmouth. He didn't raise me, and fuck my father."

The Last Train to Siena

Riccardo had nearly escaped the apartment when he stepped on the loose floorboard. It always creaked—the hidden voice of the flat, he thought—and soon his wife appeared, fingering the loose thread of her faded black housedress.

"Where are you going?" she asked.

Riccardo tried to smile. "Signora Pistilli on Via Monte Santo locked her self out of her apartment again."

The morning sun leaked in through a slit in the shutters, illuminating particles of dust floating around Maria's body. She hadn't showered, and her dark hair sat tangled above her face. Despite all that had happened, Riccardo still found his wife extraordinarily beautiful, a woman capable of transforming everyday images—dust, light, hair—into something moving and permanent, like the frescoes little Carlo showed him in his history books. "I didn't hear the phone," Maria said.

"Her son ran over," Riccardo lied. "With the ugly face?"

"I didn't hear the door."

Riccardo showed his wife his battered toolbox.

"You're the worst liar I've ever met in my life," she said. "Amalia and Pasquale arrive at three. You're still picking them up, right?"

"Of course."

"I can depend on you, right? You promise you won't get drunk, right?"

"Honey, please."

They stared into each other's eyes, and Riccardo wondered how many times they had lied to each other across twenty-nine years of marriage. Not just the big lies, the ones that let everyone go on living, but the smaller fibs like this, the minor lies that neither of them believed for even a second. He wanted to pluck a dust mite from the air and slide it into his pocket, and he wanted to ask Maria to reconsider, to not drag Amalia and Pasquale and even Carlo—just a boy in short pants!—into their pain, the darkness adults cultivate as life beats on and on and on, long after the climax. But he couldn't articulate this to his wife, so he kissed her cheek and left the apartment, eager as always for the morning drink that might jumpstart his day.

• • •

Trattoria di Nando was a trattoria in name only. Riccardo had never seen anyone reading a menu, and the only meal people ordered—perhaps once a month if the moon was full—was the most pathetic panino in the world, prosciutto and arugula in a roll harder than the dusty floorboards beneath their boots. Nando's didn't even have a sign out front. You just had to know it was there, to turn down the cramped alley of Via Faiti and descend an unmarked staircase, entering through a door that looked like it would open into a boiler room. There, in a windowless bunker like one of Mussolini's bomb shelters, was Trattoria di Nando, a charmless operation catering to the biggest winos of Prati, a neighborhood on the outskirts of Rome. Riccardo nodded at Ugo behind the bar—his brother Nando had died during the War, and Ugo opened the trattoria in his honor. Three other regulars sat at their own individual tables, reading *la Repubblica* and working through the first liter of wine of the day. Riccardo knew it was their first because the atmosphere was so dead, the underground cold and refreshing. In a few hours, they'd become the best of friends, spinning beautiful dreams that would power them through at least the rest of their afternoons. But until drunkenness took over, it was a depressing if familiar sight, and Riccardo felt thankful he'd had the wisdom to steal a few glugs from the nocino he hid in the closet that served as his office.

Riccardo ordered a liter of table wine from Ugo and sat alone in a corner. The only light pulsed down from a fluorescent tube that flickered every few minutes. He could hear the other men shifting as Ugo fiddled with his radio dial, the fuzzed over melody of an old Domenico Modugno song filling space. Riccardo set his toolbox next to his boots and began the work of becoming drunk. This always involved calculations, and he resisted using the little notebook and square carpenter's pencil he carried everywhere. It was noon. He'd already consumed what amounted to one drink of the nocino. He had to drive his rusted Fiat 1100 to Termini Station to pick up his daughter and son-in-law at three. How much could he drink in the meantime? Two liters of wine? Three? He wasn't worried about Carlo. His son never judged Riccardo no matter how drunk he became. If he slurred and stumbled, Carlo called him "Silly Daddy," and this seemed to Riccardo the finest term of endearment he'd ever earned in his life. Amalia, unfortunately, took after her mother.

The first liter went down systematically. Riccardo drank quickly and reminded himself to take another sip every other minute even if he didn't necessarily want one. He was on a schedule. And as the red wine finally began to do its work, Riccardo ordered a second liter, attracting the attention of Alberto Talarico, another pro drunk who frequented Nando's each morning. Riccardo had known Alberto—like everyone gathered in Nando's—for so long that they barely even seemed like they were different people. The neighborhood was all-knowing and all-seeing, consumed by a foaming sea of gossip that washed over all. Riccardo knew, for example, that Alberto cheated on his wife daily with the Milanese schoolteacher who lived on Piazza Mazzini, that he'd been too cowardly to join the uprising against the Nazi occupation thirty years earlier, that he was ill with gout and wasted his meager income as a plumber on visits to medicinal waters that solved nothing. Riccardo had heard similar tales about Ugo and everyone else at the trattoria, and what bothered him after all these years—like gristle behind a molar—was that they all had to pretend they didn't know anything. They could gesture to, allude to, even slightly joke about their problems, but they could never acknowledge the hidden truths that were no longer hidden, the faux-invisible burdens dragged behind them since adolescence.

"Riccardo." Alberto rubbed his shoulder and gestured at the nearby chair with his empty glass. "May I join you?"

This finagling for a free drink was ubiquitous in Nando's. The trattoria and neighborhood-at-large attracted a certain crowd—men who worked with their hands, men forced as children into Mussolini's avanguardisti, men who would never feel comfortable monetarily in their lives. Riccardo was a locksmith and occasional repairman, and he too had wandered table to table, not exactly begging for one more glass. Alberto had poured him countless free glasses over the years and would do so again. His request was merely a formality.

Riccardo refilled Alberto's glass and studied his face. His nose was stained red from his many misadventures in Nando's, and he watched Alberto struggle to sit in the chair, shifting awkwardly from buttock to buttock. Riccardo wanted to believe it was gout but feared it was simply old age. They'd grown up together during fascism, and now, just barely in their fifties, had been ground up by decades of stooping in their neighbors' apartments. He didn't want to believe he looked like Alberto but knew he likely did, that when he looked in the mirror he didn't see himself clearly. What he saw reflected there was the nest of self-illusions he'd stitched over his face, one after another, year after year, until he had fashioned himself into someone else entirely.

At first, Riccardo and Alberto spoke of inconsequential subjects—the weather, Rome's chances in the Coppa Italia, rumors of Silvani's daughter running off with some thug from Sicily. And when Alberto suggested they share a third liter of wine—he'd pay him back later, of course—what could Riccardo do but accept, redoing the calculations in his head, guessing that an extra half-liter wouldn't make much difference at this point, that he could sober up by scarfing down a sandwich at Termini. Riccardo ordered a third liter and refilled their glasses, but when Alberto produced a toothpick and pressed it to the back of his mouth, Riccardo sensed something was wrong, that the plumber had sprung a trap and was now ready to pounce.

"So," Alberto began, "Pia tells me Amalia and her northern husband are visiting?"

Pia was Alberto's wife, a woman ten years their junior who spent her days leaning out her window and gossiping with people who strolled past.

"Yes," Riccardo told him.

"What for?"

Ugo tuned the radio to some modern station, and Riccardo didn't recognize the song with its blazing guitars and thudding bass line. He checked his watch. It was nearly two. "Just to say hello. They miss Carlo."

This was obviously a lie. Since marrying a Genoese accountant three years earlier, his daughter had only returned once, for Christmas. Alberto leaned forward, grinning, and Riccardo understood his mistake, that he'd provided the perfect opening. "I'm sure she misses her brothers."

"Brother," Riccardo corrected. "Brother."

"Oh, my mistake."

And they sat there without speaking until the third liter of red wine was gone.

• • •

The first time Riccardo saw Maria was a moment of clarity that forged a path out of his seemingly endless adolescence. He was twenty years old, and she wasn't much younger, walking with her arms crossed along Via Luigi Settembrini, squawking parrots above, tram tracks on one side, two Nazis laughing on the other. Curfew started in less than an hour, and Riccardo immediately noticed the soldiers sizing her up, though in some ways he was no better. He felt devastated by her size, the compact bird-like features of her body, how malnourished everyone was then, how difficult it was to put on weight. Riccardo had fooled around with the local resistance but had accomplished little beyond running vegetables to a holed-up shack of freedom fighters in La Pisana. The Americans had already liberated Naples, and it was just a matter of time, he assured himself.

Riccardo picked up his stride and walked closer to Maria. "Excuse me, signora," he tried. "May I walk you home?"

Her eyes were closed, and her upturned nose pointed to the air, as if she would soon fly away from this place. "I don't need anyone to walk me home."

He gestured to the Nazis behind them. "Maybe I do."

In the end, she walked Riccardo to his apartment on Via Monte Pertica—blocks away from where they would spend the rest of their lives—where he lived with his mother suffering from lumbago brought on by her husband's death during Italy's invasion of Africa. Riccardo invited Maria inside for polenta and—since rations were scarce and entire neighborhoods had been caved in by bombs—she accepted.

Although they were bound by curfew and the watchful eyes of the German invaders goose-stepping down the streets, Riccardo and Maria went unsupervised by their mothers. They met in parks and church basements, at Maria's when her mother went food shopping, in the shared room Riccardo rented with four other friends for exactly this purpose. What Riccardo discovered about Maria during these many excursions was a surprising inner quality, a toughness like a steel rod. Unflappable during blackout drills, during bombings while they huddled in underground shelters, during raids where Nazis hunted down suspected communists. She seemed to Riccardo constructed from marble, a Bernini come to life. Even at twenty he felt like a boy and feared he would remain a child forever. Maria was younger than him but carried herself like a blade, like she had already seen everything, and he admired this and found himself turned on in a way he'd never experienced before, in both body and soul. When they finally made love for the first time pressed against the stone walls of an underground shelter during a cloudless afternoon, he knew he would love Maria forever and follow her happily into the grave.

His mistake, however, was telling her this. It had just ended, and Riccardo had barely pulled out in time, finishing on her ripped stocking. Maria sat on a dirty cot and rubbed her ruined stocking as her future husband proclaimed everlasting love. "You should know I'm pregnant," she said.

Riccardo was not experienced with women. He'd slept with two prostitutes at the urging of his friends, and he'd made it quickly with Gianna Borgiani in the bathroom of Cinema Gloria in the earliest days of the occupation, after Mussolini was captured and the destruction of the city felt inevitable. For one brief and tantalizing moment, Riccardo believed he'd impregnated Maria, that somehow she could sense changes at the molecular level of her body. A moment passed, and he understood the truth. She was rail thin, and it didn't seem possible.

"By who?" he whispered in the dark.

"Don't ever ask me that again."

He didn't. And he stayed with her as she began to show, as her mother tried and failed to keep her inside so no one would learn the truth. But news of Maria's pregnancy and the queer timing spread quickly throughout Prati, so widespread that Riccardo couldn't stand in line for bread without hearing snickering behind his back. It wasn't uncommon in those days, when the streets were full of Nazis, when it felt like the apocalypse had come to flush Rome down the Tiber once and for all. And after Maria delivered the baby, she asked Riccardo just one thing, a task that would decisively prove his love. "Bring him to the nuns in Siena."

You must remember that Riccardo was hopelessly in love. He knew in the furthest reaches of himself that if Maria asked him to kill the baby, he would. So after Rome was liberated and the railway opened up, Riccardo boarded a train to Siena with the still unnamed baby in his arms—five months old now!—and abandoned him to the nuns. It felt like both the beginning and end of Riccardo's life, and, in almost every way that mattered, it was.

They were married soon after and quickly had a daughter, Amalia, followed ten years later by a surprise, Carlo. They never told them about their half brother a four-hour train ride north and never spoke about him even in private, even though everyone in Prati knew, even though they saw the sneers—both real and imagined—everywhere they went. With each new year, Maria secluded herself more and more inside their apartment, shuttering the windows, warning her children not to make too many friends, to never endure a cross word said against the family. Once, after a rare Saturday when Maria drank too much wine, she told Riccardo that Prati wasn't really a neighborhood. It was a forest of unblinking eyes and if she left the apartment she would be stripped bare and consumed for all those ghouls to see. Riccardo didn't know what to say and wished he could produce the twenty-year-old Maria to put her adult incarnation at ease.

That might have been the end of everything, but then one day Riccardo received a letter from a high school math teacher in Bologna claiming to be his son. Riccardo hid this from his wife and slipped the included photo in his wallet. He'd studied it so often since that the oil of his fingers had warped it. Aldo Della Scalla did not look Italian, and this frightened Riccardo most of all. Blond hair and blue eyes with skin the texture of cream. He looked German, and for the very first time, Riccardo wondered if his wife had been impregnated by a Nazi. It had happened to many, many women. He'd heard stories. Any madness could have happened during the occupation. He once saw a dog eating a dead child in the street!

It was Maria who discovered the second letter, and she screamed at Riccardo after he returned home from Nando's. Aldo demanded a reply from his parents, and Riccardo suggested they give him one. Maria said nothing, then turned on the burner and held Aldo's second picture to the flame, burning her fingers in the process.

In the end, it was the third letter that proved most damaging, when Aldo explained that he'd hired a private detective to research the family. He knew about Amalia in Genoa and little Carlo now too. And if his parents refused to respond, Aldo threatened to reach out to his half-siblings next. Maria called Amalia immediately and said she needed to return to Prati as soon as possible, that week ideally. Riccardo overheard this from his closet/workspace, and a deep relief flooded his chest, like parts of him long dead had been massaged back to life. His wife hung up, and Riccardo joined her in the bedroom, stroking her hand gently. He still loved her, still wanted her, still found her so beautiful and stoic and strong. He needed Maria to live.

Maria stared at him, and a darkness swept over her face. They had lived together as man and wife for almost thirty years, had raised a daughter and were in the process of bringing up a son. He'd spent more time with her than anyone else he'd ever met, yet he knew in that moment that he would never understand her, that he would forever be imprisoned in the cage of his own mind. "We're going to tell them what happened," she said, "but they cannot under any circumstances acknowledge this man."

"Maria—"

"We're not going to acknowledge him. Not today. Not ever."

He braced himself on the bed. He sympathized with everything his wife had endured, the lack of options, the unwarranted shame. But to bring their own children into their lie, to ask them to keep it spinning, to prevent them from meeting their own blood . . . it was more than he could take. "We can't ask them to lie," he pleaded like a child.

"It's not a lie," she said, determined like in the old days. "It's our truth."

• • •

Now it was time to tell his children about Aldo, and Riccardo was too drunk to drive. He stood outside Nando's under the dazzling sun and accepted the truth—he'd have to walk to the subway and ride the rest of the way to Termini Station, that he'd have to help his daughter and son-in-law carry their bags the whole way back, that Amalia would immediately know he was drunk when he admitted the 1100 wasn't parked outside. He couldn't imagine any way around it, so he buried his hands in his pockets and began walking to the Lepanto stop. Via Monte Zebio was a tree-lined avenue surrounded by apartments, windows open to the sunshine, and Riccardo could feel Maria's forest of unblinking eyes looking down upon him, aware of all he had done and all he had failed to do.

It was only five stops from Lepanto to Termini, but Riccardo hated entering the grand station from underground among throngs of people carrying suitcases instead of strolling through the great glass doors along the front. Somehow, he'd arrived thirty minutes early and decided there was no point in trying to appear sober anymore. He stood under the mechanical timetable and chose a bar with a few open stools because of the pleasing pyramid of Strega bottles behind the mustachioed clerk in paper hat. He hadn't enjoyed a Strega in so long—so sweet, then shockingly bitter despite its candy yellow color—and sidled up to the bar and ordered one glass and then another and another.

Riccardo grew drunker and drunker, watching people pour in and out of the platform. He felt like a stone in a river—everyone was moving but him. On the timetable, he found Amalia's train arriving from Genoa, and as he scanned the other arrivals and departures—for Naples, Florence, Pisa, Turin—he spotted a train leaving for Siena at three. Something about reading "Siena" printed on the mechanical placard hollowed Riccardo's stomach, and he remembered that other train ride three decades earlier, when he'd been a young man transformed by the occupation, how he cradled the nameless baby in his arms and boarded a train for the first time in his life. All these years later, and he hadn't left Rome since, not even to visit Amalia in Genoa. It wasn't that he felt frightened, and he knew he'd make that journey once she had a child. But Riccardo had never seen the point in leaving before, not really.

A man sat down next to him, and Riccardo immediately knew he too was drunk. He held onto the bar to keep steady and ordered two Stregas at once. They were the only two customers who hadn't bothered ordering a sandwich or at least some snacks.

Riccardo watched the man guzzle his first drink and then his second. He ordered a third and a fourth from the bartender and during the wait turned to Riccardo and asked, "Where you headed, pal?"

He spoke before he could think. "Siena."

The drunk man nodded. "Siena? I'm from Siena!" He flagged down the bartender and ordered another Strega for Riccardo. "My treat. What brings you to Siena?"

"I'm going to visit my son," Riccardo explained.

"That right?" the drunk asked. "Cause for a celebration then," he said, raising the Strega to his lips.

They toasted Riccardo's impending visit, and then a beat passed before the drunk slapped him on the shoulder and pointed to the timetable. "You better get moving, pal. Your train's leaving."

Before he could explain it even to himself, Riccardo rose from his unsteady stool and walked under the timetable onto the platform. Amalia's train from Genoa would arrive at Platform 17, but the train bound for Siena was already parked at Platform 9. He watched men and women funneling in that direction, queuing up to enter the train. He followed them, aware that the inspector only checked your ticket once you were midway through your trip, that no one could stop him from boarding. He climbed up into the train and sat in an empty row by the window. He was drunk, but he allowed himself to believe that somehow he could avoid the inspector's ticket check, that he would be allowed to ride undisturbed all the way to Siena, that he would get off there and return to the hospital and find Maria's baby exactly as he'd left him, and then at long last everything would be righted and he and his wife would finally know peace.

• • •

In 1946, Riccardo boarded the last train to Siena, a fussy baby squirming in his arms. He sat in an empty row by the window and, as the train pushed off from the platform, watched a woman enter the car, huffing and puffing, sweat on her brow. She wore a wide-brimmed hat and was carrying a red suitcase, and Riccardo guessed she was in her forties, an upper-class housewife probably married to some fascist who had managed to avoid both death and jail. Midforties felt ancient to Riccardo, just twenty-one years old, and he knew for certain he would never grow old, that his youth would spiral outward forever and ever until the sweet collapse of time.

The woman sat next to him, the vast aisle between them. She stole glances at Riccardo and the baby, how he rocked him on his knee, sang a little melody, tickled his toes, anything to convince him to stop crying.

"He needs to burp," she said.

"Excuse me?" Riccardo asked.

"Whack him on his back."

Riccardo did as he was told, gently patting the nameless baby on his back. As the woman predicted, he burped and then turned quiet. Riccardo marveled at this woman, at the secret magic everyday people possessed. "How did you know that?" he asked.

"I've raised three," she said with a smile. "Is he your son?"

Riccardo sat rigid in his chair as the sprawl of Rome outside his window was replaced by ancient ruins, green fields, the rundown shacks that until only recently had housed the haggard resistance. He looked at the baby, placated now, and wondered if he would remember his face in a week, a month, a year. He slid his finger into the baby's hand and felt him squeeze. "He's my son," he told the woman. "He's my son."

Acknowledgments

A full list of acknowledgments would double the length of this book, so I'll try to be brief. Thank you to Theresa Beckhusen for building a life and community with me. Thanks to my parents for their support. Thanks to a lifetime of lovely writing teachers in Janine Wetter, Tom Bailey, Gary Fincke, Karla Kelsey, Chuck Kinder, Cathy Day, and Irina Reyn. Endless thanks to the Snake House Film Society. Thanks to my wonderful family of writers including Robert Yune, Katie Coyle, Geoff Peck, David James Keaton, Chris Lee, Adam Reger, Steve Gillies, Brian Oliu, Tasha Coryell, and Liz Morris. Thanks to Christopher Castellani and Nathan Hill for blurbing this book. Thanks to the 2022 Autumn House Fiction Prize judge, Venita Blackburn, for selecting this manuscript and blurbing the book. Thanks to my agent Andrianna deLone for her guidance, support, and reassurance. Thanks to Autumn House editors Christine Stroud and Mike Good for pushing *Neorealist* toward its finest incarnation. Thanks to Joel W. Coggins for designing this beautiful collection—our second professional collaboration! Thanks always to Martin Scorsese the Cat. And a deeply felt thank you to the following magazines where these stories originally appeared:

"Her Final Nights" in *Story Magazine*

"The Complete Oral History of Monkey High School" in *Yemassee*

"Do I Amuse You?" in *Always Crashing*

"Take It Out of Me" in *Another Chicago Magazine*

"Mamma-draga" in *VIA: Voices in Italian Americana*

"The Faith Center" in *Waxwing*

"The Absolutely True Autobiography of Tony Rinaldi, the Man Who Changed Pro Wrestling Forever" in *Indiana Review*

"The Last Train to Siena" in *Prairie Schooner*